# SHANI

## *HER ADVENTURES*
## *BEYOND THE SAMBATYON*

*by*

### *SHIMON BAKON*

*and*

### *PATRICIA BERLYN*

*EN-GEDI BOOKS*

ZICHRON-YA'AKOV
ISRAEL
2000

Shani – Her Adventures Beyond The Sambatyon
Copyright ® 1998 by Shimon Bakon
ISBN: 965-90235-0-2
Layout: Benjie Herskowitz
Cover Illustration by Gila Gilad

EN-GEDI BOOKS

Printed in Israel

# Contents

Chapter 1

# The Land of Beyond-Sambatyon

Who knows where the Land of Beyond-Sambatyon lies? It is the last of the unexplored places on earth. It is not shown on any map, and few people even know that it exists. It is a place of wonders that can be found nowhere else. In Beyond-Sambatyon you can be a guest in the palace of Queen Shabbat. You can hold conversations with beasts that you know about but never expected to meet, and watch the combat of the two mightiest of creatures. You can sail on the most famous of all ships, to a land where gold grows on trees, and be borne through the air by a horse that has no peer. You can find the Kingdom of the Lost Tribes, and can seek the most precious of all hidden Treasures. You can meet Af-Bri, the giant Prince of the Rains and Winds.

That is, you can have these adventures if you can reach the Land of Beyond-Sambatyon. It is surrounded by a ring of jagged mountains that pierce the clouds. It is impossible to climb them, because icy winds blast with such fury that they sweep away everything in their path. You cannot fly over them, because there are strange magnetic forces in the rocks. If an aircraft approaches them, its instruments will not work and it must veer away.

Even if you could somehow make your way over these mountains, you still could not enter the Land of Beyond-Sambatyon. All around its borders flows the River Sambatyon, whose waters churn and swirl and roar, and hurl up huge stone boulders both day and night. They fly skyward and then crash back down with a tremendous splash and dreadful din. This deadly hail would fall on any boat or swimmer.

There is not a moment of quiet until the sun begins to set on Friday evening. Then, just before the start of Shabbat, the waters lie calm and the stones sink and rest on the riverbed. At the same time, a wall of flames rises from the depths and burns silently and steadily through all the Holy Day of Rest.

Thousands of years ago, scholars heard tales about this mysterious river, and wrote them down in their books. They never knew how to find it, or how anyone could cross it and reach the Land of Beyond-Sambatyon.

Yet there is one secret way to cross the River Sambatyon. Elijah the Prophet knows it, but he will reveal it only if he befriends somebody who has a very good and special reason to visit Beyond-Sambatyon.

Shani did have a very good and special reason. That is why Elijah trusted her with the secret. That is why she was able to make her journey all the way from America to Beyond-Sambatyon . . .

*Chapter 2*

# A Visit from Elijah

Shani was nine years old, going on ten, at the time of her great adventure. She was a little lonely then. Since her brother Dani was born, Ima had to take care of a baby besides all the other things she did, and she seldom had much time just for Shani.

Dani was cute, but so far there was little he could do except cry, often in the middle of the night to wake Shani from sleep. Still, whenever he made a tiny sweet smile and gurgled at her as though he knew her, she had to give him a hug and a kiss.

One night she could not fall asleep. She thought about the Pessah they had just celebrated. She could recall the Seder as though she were seeing it all over again — many family members gathered at the long table — the Seder plate set with the special foods — the silver goblet filled with wine for Elijah the Prophet. When the door was opened to welcome him, she kept her gaze fixed on that goblet. Had she really felt a little ripple of breeze cross the room? Had the wine really stirred? She had been so sure of it, that she had cried out, "Look, Ima, Abba, everyone! Elijah has tasted his wine!"

Cousin Adam at once said, "I saw it, too." He was almost a year older than Shani and never liked her to know anything that he did not know better. Great-Aunt Sophie gave the tight little smile of grown-ups who think children are being childish, but Ima and Abba gave her real smiles, bright with love.

Thinking about Elijah led her to think about the close of Shabbat earlier that evening. As always, she had held the braided candle for Abba as he performed the *havdalah* ceremony that marked the end of the special day of Shabbat and the start of a new week. Then they had sung a song about Elijah the Prophet. As her lids finally grew heavy with sleep, she saw the flickering light of the candle and heard the song.

She whispered, "Please, please, come again."

૨૦ ૨૦ ૨૦

Spring that year was too hot and too dry. Summer was worse. Month after month went by and not a drop of rain fell on the parched earth. The sun blazed down hotly all day, every day. Rivers shrank to shallow brooks and streams dried up altogether. Grass turned yellow and died. Soil was packed hard or crumbled and gritty. Fruits on the trees shriveled and rotted, stalks of wheat and corn in the fields slumped with drooping heads. There were no flowers. Even dandelions turned to dust. Small animals found little water to lap up, and the songs of the birds were stilled.

Scientists called meteorologists, who were supposed to understand all about weather, were at a loss. They studied their instruments, and made calculations, and muttered and shook their heads. Even the cleverest of them could not find a reason for the long drought or guess when it might end.

The levels of the reservoirs dropped lower and lower. People were warned to use as little water as possible, so gardens and parks died, streets went unwashed, cars were dusty. Before long, there might not even be enough to drink. Everyone was worn down by the heat and anxiety. Tired children did not care to play, and grown-ups went about with long faces. They became cross and cranky, let their work go undone, and broke into sharp quarrels for little reason.

Shani longed to do something to make things better, but what could anyone do to make it rain? Of all her books, the one she loved best was a collection of stories from the Bible, that she read over and over again. She remembered a story about a land that was perishing from lack of rain, and how one man knew how to save it. That man had been Elijah the Prophet.

After that, every evening when she recited the *Shema* at bedtime, she added, "Oh, please, we need Elijah to help us, too."

One night, as she was reciting this plea there was suddenly a man standing over her and looking straight down at her. He had thick hair and a beard, and wore a leather tunic and a mantle of rough wool. He looked strange, almost fierce, but she felt not the slightest fear of him.

He smiled at her, and asked, "Why have you called for me, Shani? What do you want of me?"

She answered him eagerly, without any hesitation or shyness. She told him all about the long, terrible heat with no rain, how people and animals were suffering, how all growing things were dying. Then she asked, "Prophet Elijah, can you help us?"

"You, yourself, can help, Shani. Are you are willing to undertake a hard task?"

"I'll try. What can I do?"

"Do you know of Af-Bri?"

She shook her head.

"He is Prince of the Rains and Winds. His name is in the prayer for rain on the festival of Shemini Atzereth. He can send the rains forth around the world. Will you go to seek him, and try to persuade him to send them here?"

"Yes! I'll go! Where can I find him?"

"On the highest peak of the highest mountain in the faraway land of Beyond-Sambatyon."

"Where is that? How can I get there?"

Elijah seemed to be considering the problem. Then he opened a small sack tied to his belt and drew out a bronze whistle with odd symbols on it. He put it on the table beside Shani's bed.

"When you start your journey, blow once on this whistle. The bird called Duchipat will hear it and come to carry you to the shore of the ocean.

"Then, blow twice on the whistle. The creature called Leviathan will hear it and come to carry you across the ocean.

"Then, blow three times on the whistle. Ashmodai, King of the Demons, will hear it. Ages ago, King Solomon bound Ashmodai in chains of gold, but I will let him go free just long enough to carry you over the mountains to the River Sambatyon."

"How long will it take me to get there?"

"Tomorrow is Friday. If you start out in the morning, you should reach the Sambatyon just before sunset and the start of Shabbat. You must cross it before Shabbat begins.

11

"That will bring you into the Land of Beyond-Sambatyon, which is ruled by Queen Shabbat. She will tell you how to reach Af-Bri. The way will be hard, but I believe that you will not give up until you find him."

Elijah was silent for a moment, then went on. "The River Sambatyon does not allow anyone to cross it, except by one way that is a deep secret. I will tell it to you now. You must never, never tell it to anyone else."

The Prophet's voice dropped to a whisper, and Shani had to listen very carefully to understand and remember all that he said. Then the whisper faded into silence. As suddenly as he had appeared, Elijah had disappeared.

When she awoke in the morning, Shani thought it had all been a dream. Then she saw the whistle on her bedside table.

"It wasn't a dream!" she cried aloud.

*Chapter 3*

# The Journey to Beyond-Sambatyon

S hani told Ima and Abba that she was going to take a journey, so they would not worry about her while she was away. When they sat together at the breakfast table, she repeated every word of her talk with Elijah the Prophet — except for the secret.

"That was a very nice dream," Ima said.

"It wasn't a dream. It was real. Truly it was. Here's the whistle."

Abba took it up, turned it over and over and said, "It looks very old. There seems to be writing on it, but I can't make it out. Where did you get this, Shani?"

"Elijah gave it to me," she repeated patiently. "To help me get to the Land of Beyond-Sambatyon."

"Is your friend Miriam going with you?" Ima asked.

"No, I must go alone. I'll be safe. Elijah will look after me." She gazed at them anxiously. What could she do if her parents would not let her go?

Ima said only, "Have a good time. Don't cross the highway, the traffic is dangerous."

"I don't need to go near the highway."

"And remember, we have to make ready for Shabbat. You can frost the cake."

"This Shabbat I'll be with the Queen in Beyond-Sambatyon. I'm sure I'll be home before next Shabbat."

"The Queen's cake won't be as good as your mother's," Abba said with a laugh, and gave her a quick hug. "Now, I must be going."

After he left, Shani told Ima, "I have a long way to go. I'm starting now."

"All right, dear. Be careful, and don't get overheated."

Shani was relieved that they understood. Sometimes grown-ups were slow to catch on about important things.

She did not know what to do to prepare for the journey, so she decided not to prepare for it all. She just put a candy bar into her pocket, in case she got hungry while going over the ocean and up the mountain. Then she went to Dani's room, bent over his crib, and said, "I'll tell you all about it when I get home."

៹ ៹ ៹

Shani went outside to an open field behind the garden of their house, drew in her breath and blew one hard puff on the whistle. There was no sound, and she thought it was not working. Soon, however, a broad shadow was cast on the dry, cracked earth. She looked up. It was a bird. She had never imagined a bird could be so huge.

It glided down to a smooth landing beside her and spoke in a clear, ringing voice.

15

"I am Duchipat. Sit on my back and hold on tightly. We will fly high and fast, but have no fear. I'll take you safely to the shore of the sea."

Shani climbed onto a nearby pile of rocks to reach Duchipat's back. She clung to thick feathers as they lifted off and rose high into the sky. Despite Duchipat's promise, she was scared at first, but soon she relaxed and looked down.

They soared over towns and countryside, and rivers like long blue ribbons. Now and then they overtook a speeding train. From so far above, the tallest buildings and longest trains seemed like toys. It was so much fun that she was a bit sorry when they reached a sweep of sandy beach and the ocean beyond. Duchipat landed gently and Shani slid down onto the sand.

"Thank you. Goodbye," she called, and waved as the great bird rose and flew off.

"Now, I'll blow the whistle twice and see what happens."

Again there was no sound, but this time she was sure the whistle was working. She watched the sea and saw mighty waves rolling toward the beach. The waters split and an immense form appeared, glistening green and gold, its slapping tail beating up breakers as high as a house. It streaked toward her until the water was too shallow for its bulk, and spoke in a deep, rumbling voice.

"I am Leviathan. Sit on my back and hold on tight. We will swim far and fast, but have no fear. I'll take you safely to the far shore of the sea."

Shani waded into the rippling water and clambered onto Leviathan's back. She clasped a broad neck as they cut through the ocean. Despite Leviathan's promise, she was scared at first, but soon she relaxed and looked around and down into the depths.

They were skimming over reefs of twisted corals and schools of darting fishes and strange things with slithering tentacles. Dolphins frolicked beside them, but they could not keep up with Leviathan. It was so exciting that she was a bit sorry when they reached the other side of the ocean. Leviathan brought her close to shore, where she slid down and splashed her way to dry land.

"Thank you. Goodbye," she called, and waved as the great creature plunged back into the deep.

She looked all around her. There was no sandy beach here, but only sharp stones. In the distance, steep craggy mountains stood with their peaks hidden in thick mist. Shani felt how alone she was in this bare and empty place, and shuddered.

"If Elijah sent me here, it must be okay," she said out loud to herself. "I'll blow the whistle three times and see what happens."

Again there was no sound, but soon there was a noise like the roar of a tornado. A spinning swirl of darkness appeared overhead and settled to the ground. As the spinning slowed and came to a stop, she could see a figure wrapped in a long black cloak. It was a man, with the claws and sharp wings of some hideous fowl. He stared at her, with a glare like burning coals. Shani knew this must be Ashmodai, King of the Demons.

He spoke in a voice like a roll of thunder. "Why have I been called here?"

Shani tried to hide her fear and disgust, but her own voice shook when she said, "Please, take me to the River Sambatyon." She hastily added, "Elijah the Prophet says you should."

Without a word, he snatched her up and leaped into the air. Higher and higher they went, his black cloak billowing like a sail in the wind. She grabbed onto it, and did not dare to look down. Only

17

once she took a peek, and below were sharp pinnacles of rock pointed up at her like daggers. She wished this flight would be over quickly, but it seemed a long time before Ashmodai suddenly let her drop onto hard earth.

"Thank you," she said. It was a rule to thank anyone who did something for you, and she supposed that went even for a Demon King. She did not say goodbye or wave as he vanished in a puff of black smoke.

She found herself on flat ground. She looked one way, and there stood the range of mountains she had just crossed. She looked the other way — and there it was! She had come so far to seek it, she could scarcely believe that she was standing beside the River Sambatyon. Its turbulent waters rushed along, carrying swirling sands with it. Boulders flew up, clashed in the air and hurtled down again with a fearsome noise. Surely anyone who ventured onto that river would be crushed. She could not see across to the other side, but she knew it was the boundary of the Land of Beyond-Sambatyon.

The sun was near to the horizon. She glanced at the watch that Abba had given her as a Hanukkah gift. There was only half an hour left before the start of Shabbat. She must cross at once. She did exactly as Elijah had taught her . . .

ে৯ ে৯ ে৯

Shani stood on soft, sweet-smelling grass. She looked behind her at the River Sambatyon. The waters were tranquil now and the boulders had ceased to leap and fall. A high wall of flickering red flames blazed and barred the way across.

She looked ahead of her, and found a path bordered by trees. She followed it toward a splendid building of delicately shaded stone and tinted marbles. Surely this must be the palace of the Queen!

As she ran eagerly toward it, bronze doors swung open and two girls came out. They seemed to be about the same age as Shani and were very pretty. They were so much alike that the only way to tell them apart was that one wore a white ribbon in her hair and the other a blue one. The moment Shani saw them, she felt that she had always known them and that they had always been her dear friends.

"Welcome, Shani," they said together.

"This is my sister, Shamor," said one.

"This is my sister, Zachor," said the other.

"We are the twin daughters of Queen Shabbat."

"She has sent us to greet you."

Shani was so happy, she had to laugh. "I know what your names mean in Hebrew. *Shamor* is Observe and *Zachor* is Remember — like the commandments Observe Shabbat and Remember Shabbat."

The twins also laughed with pleasure.

"Come and see how we Observe and Remember here," Zachor said.

Through the open doors Shani could hear a voice singing most beautifully.

"I know that song! It's *'Lecha Dodi,'* that we sing to welcome Shabbat."

"Prince Lecha-Dodi himself is singing it," Shamor told her. "He is one of our mother's court."

"So is Prince Kiddush," Zachor added. "You will hear him sing later."

Walking between her two old-new friends, Shani entered the palace of Queen Shabbat

Chapter 4

# Shabbat Shalom

S hani woke to the sound of music different from any she had ever heard. It was both delicate and strong, with many strains blending into a strange and exquisite harmony. She was so enchanted by it that at first she wanted only to listen, and did not even look around the room. When she did, she was confused, for this was not her own room where she awoke every morning.

Then she remembered that she was now in Beyond-Sambatyon, in the palace of Queen Shabbat. Shamor and Zachor had brought her straight to this room, and told her it would be hers for as long as she was a guest here. A new dress had been laid out for her to change quickly for Shabbat dinner that was about to begin. She had been so weary after the journey, that the evening that followed seemed to her like a dream. Now she was not sure how much she recalled was real and how much dream.

Surely, Queen Shabbat could not have been a dream. She was so beautiful, stately and serene. She wore a simple and lovely white silk gown. and a golden crown. She had spoken to Shani very kindly, and led her to a place close to her own chair at the head of the table.

There had been many other people there, who gave her a friendly welcome. Shamor and Zachor had told her who each of them was, but now she found it hard to sort them out in her memory. She could not recollect the end of the dinner at all. She was afraid that she had fallen asleep before it was over.

Shani got up, hoping to find the source of the wonderful music. She looked all about the room, but it did not seem to come from any one place. However, she did find everything that a guest might need, including new clothes that fit her perfectly.

Soon there was a light tap on the door, and when she answered the twins came in together.

"We thought you would be awake by now," Zachor said.

"I've been listening to the music. I never heard anything so lovely. Where does it come from?"

"It's the song of the morning stars," Shamor said.

"You can't see them when it's daylight," Zachor added. "But they are in the sky."

"The stars make music?" Shani was puzzled.

"Of course," Shamor answered. "We are told of them in the Book of Job: 'The morning stars sang together.'"

"What do they sing?"

"Praises to God. Listen, can't you hear?"

Shani listened very hard. Then she cried out joyfully, "Yes, yes, I can hear! They sing *kadosh, kadosh, kadosh!** Will I hear them every morning?"

---

The Hebrew word *"kadosh"* is "holy" in English.

"No, they sing only on Shabbat."

Shani thought she would not be there for next Shabbat, so she would never hear the enchanting music again. She was sad at that, but at the same time happy that she would be back with Ima and Abba and could tell them about the singing of the morning stars and the other remarkable things here.

❧ ❧ ❧

She had expected that she would go on to Af-Bri the next day, and home the day after that. Later that morning she learned it could not be so.

Queen Shabbat took her into her private parlor. Though she was so noble, she was also so warm and natural that Shani was not a bit shy with her. She felt, as with the Queen's daughters, that she had known her all her life.

"Elijah has told me  about you, Shani, and why you have come to Beyond-Sambatyon. You will enjoy your visit with us."

"I love being here, but I can't stay. I must go find Af-Bri."

"Not yet. I will tell you when to seek him."

"Can't I go tomorrow? It's awfully urgent, you know."

"I do indeed know. But Af-Bri is an odd and difficult creature. You must prove yourself first, before he will have anything to do with you."

Shani thought she had already proved herself by getting to Beyond-Sambatyon, but it might seem boastful to say so.

The Queen went on. "In the meantime, my daughters have planned some entertainment for you."

"But things are so hard at home, and my family . . ."

"I'm glad you're thinking of them, and not of the good time you can have here. Be assured, this way will work out for the best. And now, I have a little gift for you."

She took from a drawer a pocket mirror in a silver frame and gave it to Shani.

"Oh, thank you very much. It's so pretty."

"If you are ever troubled or frightened, or don't know what to do, look into the mirror. It will help you."

"Is it magic?" Shani asked, excited.

"Let us say it is very special."

The Queen arose and embraced Shani and kissed her. "Go along now with my girls. We will talk again."

ua ua ua

Shamor and Zachor were waiting for her, to take her on a tour of the palace. Shani soon ran out of words for her delight and amazement at the many lofty halls and chambers, marble floors, tapestries and hangings.

They ended in the dining room, where the Shabbat afternoon meal was being set out on a buffet. A woman so plump and round that she rolled and waddled as she walked was busily supervising.

"This is Madam Cholent," Zachor introduced her. "She is the original inventor of Shabbat cholent, that is named after her."

"I saw you last night, dearie," Madam Cholent said to Shani. "You fell asleep at the table when you had scarcely tasted a bite."

"I'm sorry," Shani said, embarrassed.

"She'll do better today," Shamor promised.

Madam Cholent was bustling about, inspecting, checking and moving things around.

"You can't imagine the responsibilities I have. All week long, I must plan and supervise cuisine fit for a Queen's table."

She began half reciting, half chanting.

> *Keep the soup hot, cover the pot*
> *Scrub tomatoes, peel potatoes*
> *After they boil, sauté in oil*
> *Simmer and brew a tangy stew*
> *Stir it and baste and take a taste*
>
> *Green peas to shell, aspic to jell*
> *Carrots to scrape, dumplings to shape*
> *Fluff up some rice and add some spice*
> *Cut out noodles by the oodles*
> *Salad to shred, to be well fed*
>
> *Beat, beat and bake a honey cake*
> *Biscuits with yeast add to the feast*
> *Pie crusts to stuff, pasties to puff*
> *Design some tarts — use all your arts*
> *Put in cherries, put in berries*
>
> *Six kinds of cheese, choose what you please*
> *Apples to pare sweeten the fare*
> *Sherbets in tints, plenty of mints*
> *Dates cut with slits, take out the pits*
> *I never shirk! I love my work!*

Now Queen Shabbat entered and took her seat at the head of the long table. Prince Lecha-Dodi, who was very handsome and elegant, sat on one side of her. Prince Kiddush, who had fine looks and a friendly smile, sat on the other. His Excellency Havdalah sat between his two sons, the sweet-faced Besamim and the ruddy Me'or-Esh. Opposite the girls were two men whom the twins introduced as Machshavah, who had a high brow and a serious look, and Ma'aseh, who was robust with a brisk manner.*

There were many other guests at the meal, but when it was done only these few and Madam Cholent gathered in the Queen's pavilion, set in the midst of flower gardens.

"We always come here on Shabbat afternoon," Shamor told Shani. "We sing, and we talk about what we have seen and done during the week."

Some of the Shabbat songs were new to Shani, especially a quick and lively tune led by Besamim and Me'or Esh. After the singing, Machshavah gave a very learned talk on some new mathematical calculations he had worked out from the Book of Numbers. It seemed to go on for quite a long time, but Shani was sure it would be very interesting if she could understand any of it.

Some of the others told stories about places they had been and things they had seen. Finally, perhaps so she should not feel left out, the Queen persuaded Shani to talk about her home and her family, and how they kept their Shabbat.

By the time the shadows of late afternoon began to fall, Shani felt that if only Ima and Abba and Dani had been there, it would have been the most perfect day of her life.

---

*'*Lecha-Dodi*' is a song to welcome Shabbat. *Kiddush* is the blessing for the wine. *Havdalah* is the ceremony to conclude Shabbat, in which *besamim* (spices) and *me'or esh* (firelight) are used. *Machshavah* (thought) and *Ma'aseh* (deed) are both in the words of the song *'Lecha-Dodi.'*

*Chapter 5*

# A Steed and His Boy

The next day, Shamor and Zachor tapped on Shani's door early in the morning.

"We're taking you to the Aharit HaYamim Zoo."*

"There's not another one like it in the whole world."

"And then we'll have a swim."

They set out right after breakfast, each carrying a basket with a picnic lunch and a bathing-suit. They crossed an open field where the only sounds were the chirping of birds and the buzzing of flying insects. Suddenly there was another sound, so unexpected that it startled Shani. It was the neigh of a horse.

She looked about and saw a large, very beautiful white stallion trotting toward her. He was drawing a small chariot made of a metal that took on a fiery sheen in the rays of the sun. A boy a few years

---

* The Hebrew words *"Aharit HaYamim"* are "The End of Days" in English. They mean the time of peace and happiness to come in the future.

28

older than Shani was standing in the chariot, but did not hold any reins. The twins called to him and waved, and he waved back.

"That's Elizur," Shamor said. "He travels a lot. I'm glad he's here so you can meet him."

As the boy came nearer, they could hear him singing.

> *O, I wonder*
> *What is yonder,*
> *So to and fro*
> *I long to go.*
>
> *This splendid steed*
> *With grace and speed,*
> *Can soar and fly*
> *Through cloud and sky.*
>
> *O'er land and sea,*
> *He carries me.*
> *We rove and roam,*
> *Then we come home.*

When he was quite close, Elizur stepped down from the chariot and walked up to them. The splendid horse, who obviously needed no driver, paced along beside him. When the pair came up to the girls, the horse neighed again, reared off the ground, and spread out a pair of broad, shimmering white wings.

"A horse with wings!" Shani cried. "How can that be?"

"This isn't just any horse," Elizur said proudly, enjoying her amazement. "This is Pega-Soos."*

"Is he yours?"

---

* The Hebrew word *"soos"* is "horse" in English.

"No, I'm his. We're friends. I look after him and he takes me everywhere I want to go. I love to travel."

"So do I," Shani said. "I've traveled in strange ways lately, but never in a chariot."

"Get in for a ride. There's room for all of you. I'll walk. Where are you going?"

"To the Zoo," Shamor said. "We were so busy admiring Pega-Soos that we didn't introduce Shani yet. She's visiting from the outside."

They clambered into the chariot, that Shani could see was very, very old and quite battered. Elizur swung himself up to ride Pega-Soos bareback.

"How did you get to Beyond-Sambatyon, Shani? By one of your strange ways of travel?"

"Three strange ways." Shani was glad to tell her tale to another traveler. When she spoke of Duchipat and Leviathan he smiled and nodded, as though he knew them himself. When she came to Ashmodai, he looked surprised and said, "You sure needed spunk for that."

Shani thought so too, and liked to hear somebody else say it, especially another adventurer.

"Now it's your turn," she said to Elizur. "Tell us how you came to be such a wanderer."

"It's a long story," he warned her, though he did not seem at all reluctant to tell it.

"Go ahead," Zachor said. "We have time enough."

"I was born in the little town of Zarephath, near the Mediterranean Sea. When I was just a baby, my mother became a widow. We were very poor. When I was still a small child, there was a fearful drought and famine in the land, and she could hardly get any food for us. At last, nothing was left but a little flour and a little olive oil.

We went to gather twigs for a fire to cook our last meal. After those few bites, we would starve to death."

Shani thought of how hard it sometimes was to wait for the next meal and wondered how it must feel to be really hungry and have no food and no hope of food.

Elizur went on with his story. "We were near the town gate when a stranger entered and came up to us. He looked strange, almost fierce, but I had no fear of him.

"He asked Mother for a drink of water. We didn't have much, but she went in the house and poured some for him. Then he asked for a piece of bread, but she had none in the house to give him. She told him we had only a bit of flour and a bit of olive oil and nothing else. When it was gone, we would die. What there was, we would share with him.

"She wept as she said that. The stranger spoke very gently to her. He promised that the flour and oil would last as long as we needed it, and it did. He stayed as a guest in a little room on the roof. Every day, Mother baked something for the three of us, and the flour and the oil never got used up. You see, this stranger was . . ."

"Don't tell me," Shani interrupted him. "I know. He's my friend, too. What happened next?"

Elizur took on a solemn and self-important look. "Then I fell very, very sick. In fact, I was as good as dead. There seemed to be not a breath of life in me. Just think how poor Mother wept then.

"So Elijah — yes, of course it was Elijah — carried me up to his room on the roof. He prayed for me and he tended me. The breath came back to me and I lived.

"Then he went away. Things got better for Mother and me, we had enough for ourselves. But I thought always of Elijah. I wanted to serve him in any way I could. I waited until I was big enough to travel alone, and then I set out to search for him.

"I went from town to town, and land to land. I asked for him everywhere. Sometimes folk had seen him, but always he had gone on his way. At last, one day as I was coming to the River Jordan, I saw him. I ran to him as fast as I could, calling to him.

"Before I could reach him, there was a great blaze in the sky that came swooping down to earth. It turned out to be this chariot, and a team of horses led by Pega-Soos, all aglow like fire. Elijah mounted into the chariot and a tremendous whirlwind lifted it up until it disappeared into the clouds. I thought I had lost him forever.

"But he knew how I had searched for him, and he didn't forget us. He brought Mother and me to Beyond-Sambatyon. We have a nice cottage not far from here. And I've been entrusted with the care of Pega-Soos. We've gone far and wide together during all these years."

"You must have lots more stories to tell," she hinted.

"Lots and lots."

She was disappointed when Shamor said, "But not another one now. This is where we turn off to the Zoo. Do you want to come with us?"

"I'd like to, but I can't. I promised to help with the arrangements for the Mock Combat today."

"What's a Mock Combat?" Shani asked.

"Come to it and see for yourself."

"Can we go?" she asked the twins.

"Yes, after the Zoo," Zachor answered. "If it takes place. Nobody knows for sure yet."

"It will take place," Elizur assured them with a grin.

*Chapter 6*

# At The Aharit HaYamim Zoo

The girls stepped down from the chariot, and Elizur mounted it. Pega-Soos reared, gave a flash of his wings, and trotted off. The three then went on their way toward the Zoo. Soon they could hear a chorus of barks and honks and hoots. Loudest of all was a piteous braying.

"That's Balaam's ass," the twins told Shani.

Past a cluster of trees they came to a small enclosed yard with a roofed stall stocked with piles of hay. Reclining in front of the stall was a most ancient donkey with grizzled coat and yellow teeth.

"What an ugly old jackass that is," Shani said.

"Don't insult me," the donkey snapped indignantly. "I'm no jackass. I'm a jenny. That's the female of the species, and therefore much wiser. Don't you agree?"

Shani was so taken aback that the animal not only understood but answered, that at first she could only nod. Then she said, "I'm very sorry. I didn't mean to hurt your feelings. Won't you please tell me about your adventure with Balaam?"

The she-ass seemed pleased with this interest in her story.

"Balaam was my human. He provided my home and food and took me for rides. He was so clever and famous that kings sent to plead for his help. But when an angel stood right in front of him, he couldn't see it.

"I recognized it right away, and had sense enough to know an angel must have a really important message. Three times I tried to alert Balaam, and three times he beat me for it. He finally woke up to the truth, but who knows what would have happened if it weren't for me?"

"What?" Shani urged her to go on.

The she-ass gave another bray, this one proud rather than piteous. "I am written up in The Book. If you want to know the rest of the story, read it. Now, if you will excuse me, it's time for my snack." She gave a farewell swish of her tail and ambled into her stall.

The girls strolled on. Shani had expected a zoo to have fences, or even cages, but there were none here. It was like a park, where all the animals roamed freely. A lamb sipping at a pond showed no fear of the big wolf padding around it. A little kid was cuddled up beside a leopard. Nearby a calf frolicked while a lion strode back and forth. A cow was chomping grass next to a bear who was licking a honeycomb.

Shamor laughed at Shani's wonderment. "You're surprised? This is just the start of the surprises."

"Don't the ferocious ones hurt the others?"

"Oh, no, never," Zachor assured her. "This zoo is the way the whole world will be at the time of *Aharit HaYamim*. Just as Isaiah the Prophet described it, you know."

Shani did not know. When she got home she would ask Abba about Isaiah the Prophet.

They sat down to rest next to the leopard, and stroked his sleek back. He flashed his fearsome fangs and purred. The tiny kid beside him squealed while he waited his turn to be petted. Shani gave him a gentle hug. Why did he remind her of Dani?

"Tell our guest whose kid you are," Zachor suggested.

This time Shani was ready to hear an animal speak.

"I was born among flocks and herds grazing in a desert land," the kid began. "One day, I wandered away from my Ima and got lost. I walked and walked and couldn't find my way back to her. I was so tired, so thirsty. I tried to find water but there was none. I gave up all hope.

"But my shepherd missed me, and searched through the wilderness until he found me. He gave me water and carried me back to Ima. He even said he was sorry he had not watched out for me more carefully. That was how my shepherd Moses showed that he was fit to become the shepherd of all Israel."

"Now I remember that story, from one of my books. Who could have dreamed I'd ever meet you."

"Oh, you have always known me very well," the kid said. He seemed to be teasing her.

"I have?" She was puzzled.

"Certainly. You sing a long song about me every year, at the end of the Seder."

Shani thought for a moment, and then laughed. "You're Chad Gadya! The Only Kid!"

She began to sing to the tune she knew so well.

*There came a cat and ate the kid . . .*
*There came a dog and bit the cat. . .*
*There came a stick and beat the dog . . .*
*There came a fire and burned the stick . . .*
*There came water and quenched the fire . . .*

She broke off, and said sadly, "Too much of it is about how the bigger and stronger bully the smaller and weaker."

"Here at Aharit HaYamim it's all different," the kid told her. He went on in a high-pitched singsong.

*There came a cat and played with the kid,*
*That's really what she did.*
*There came a dog and romped with the cat,*
*What do you think of that?*
*There came a stick and jumped with the dog,*
*Who took it for a jog.*
*There came a fire and licked at the stick,*
*Just as a joke and trick.*
*There came some water warmed by the fire,*
*And we could splash in mire.*

The girls cheered his song, then took their leave and went on with their walk. Here and there, they paused to watch the animals. A group of slender does came right up to them, and Shani held out fresh grasses for them to nibble.

By and by, they entered the woods. Shani thought she heard drums. The sound was a heavy boom by the time they came into a circular clearing. At one side of the clearing, two apes squatted on the ground slapping on big drums, beating out constantly changing rhythms. High above them, on the spreading branches of the trees, more apes swung around and around, or turned somersaults and cartwheels, or leaped through the air from branch to branch and tree to tree.

"I never saw anything like this!" Shani exclaimed. "Not even at a circus."

The nearer drummer turned toward her and said with dignity, "We are not circus apes, Miss. We are royal apes. We are King Solomon's own apes."

"His Majesty sent a fleet of his ships all the way to far off Ophir, to invite us to come to his splendid court in Jerusalem," said the second ape.

"A whole fleet just for you?"

"Well, while the crews were there they picked up a few other things, but only common stuff like gold and silver and ivory."

"And peacocks," the first ape added. "What good they are, I'm sure I don't know."

"We put on many shows for King Solomon," the other went on. "We were much admired. The Queen of Sheba once fed us herself, with the finest fruits and nuts."

"An *artiste* deserves appreciation," his comrade said.

Shani looked up again at the apes swinging and leaping to the beat of the drums.

"And you're still doing it, I see."

"It's still fun. And we have to keep in practice, in case we are ever asked to give another Command Performance."

The girls watched for a few more minutes, and applauded. The apes bowed. Then they went on their way, and the beat of the drums faded in the distance.

Farther along, they came to a lake as clear as crystal. There was a brightly striped tent, where they changed into their bathing-suits for a frolic in the sparkling water. It was great sport, that gave them great appetites, so they sat by the lake to empty their picnic baskets while their hair dried in the sun. It was such a delightful scene, she wished she could send a picture postcard of it to her friend Miriam.

While they were sitting there, a large black raven and a large white dove set down on a branch of a nearby tree. They were snapping back and forth at one another as though they were having a quarrel.

"Guess who those birds are," Shamor said.

Once more Shani thought back to her book of Bible tales. "The birds Noah sent from the ark to see if the Flood was over?"

Both the twins nodded.

She realized that she could make sense out of their noises.

"I was the one Noah sent out first," the raven croaked.

"I was the one who found the first new leaf that budded," the dove gurgled.

"And after that you deserted the ship."

"You took a nice cruise, but I had important things to do."

"What did you ever do that was important? When Elijah the Prophet fled from Queen Jezebel who wanted to kill him, and hid in the wilderness, who brought him food? You? Never! I did!"

"Do they always argue like that?" Shani asked.

"Yes," Zachor said. "They've been going on like that for ages and ages."

"They stay together most of the time," Shamor said, "so they must enjoy it."

As they watched, the two birds flew off wing to wing, still cawing and cooing their ancient feud.

Chapter 7

# The Mock Combat

It was early afternoon when they set out for the Mock Combat.
"You still haven't told me what it is," Shani reminded the twins.
"I can figure out that it must be some kind of make-believe battle. Is it like a tournament with knights?"

"It will be more like a match," Zachor said. "If there is any opponent for Behemoth."

"Who's Behemoth?"

"The strongest and mightiest creature on the earth. At least he thinks he is. To prove it, he put out a challenge to fight anyone or anything that dares to face him."

"Will one of them get hurt or killed?" Shani asked uneasily.

"Oh, no. The judges won't allow that. They'll keep score and declare a winner. That's why it's called a Mock Combat."

"Who's going to fight Behemoth?"

"We don't know. Behemoth says he'll be in the arena at one o'clock to fight any opponent."

"Maybe there won't be one," Shani said, "I guess then he'll really gloat that every creature is afraid of him."

"He surely will. But Elizur seemed certain that there will be an opponent. Maybe he knows who it is."

The site of the Mock Combat was a large arena with a sandy floor. At either end was an opening like the mouth of a tunnel. On one side was a platform where three men sat under an canopy. Beside them stood two men holding long brass trumpets.

"The judges and the heralds," Zachor said, which Shani had already guessed.

They found a place to sit on a low hillside. There were many people gathered around, and also animals from the countryside and the Zoo, all settling down to watch the show.

The heralds stepped forth, blew long gliding blasts on their trumpets, and each took a place beside one of the tunnels. The first herald blew a short toot and shouted, "The challenger! Behemoth!"

A massive hulking form rushed out of the tunnel into the arena. Behemoth gave the judges and audience a fiery look, and impatiently stomped the ground with hoofs so hard that they struck sparks.

Everyone was silent now, waiting to see if any opponent would appear. The second herald blew a short toot and shouted, "To challenge the challenger! Leviathan!"

"Leviathan!" Shani was pleased and excited. "I know him. He carried me over the sea."

But when Leviathan emerged from the other tunnel, she was puzzled and said, "That's not him. This one's smaller and not the same colors."

"This isn't your Leviathan," Shamor explained. "He never leaves the oceans. This is his youngest brother, the one who's called Baby

Leviathan. He loves adventure and he'll go anywhere to find it, even onto land."

"I didn't know there's more than one Leviathan."

"There's a whole family. King and Queen Leviathan rule all the creatures of the seas from their palace in the depths of Pan-Oceania. Baby is their littlest son."

Shani looked at the huge creature and giggled. "Some baby."

"In the Leviathan family he's still the baby. He doesn't like to be called that. He thinks he's all grown up now, but he isn't."

By that time, Baby Leviathan had reached the center of the sandy floor, nodding amiably to the crowd, and flapping his tail.

The three judges said together, "Let the combat commence."

"Just a minute, sirs, if you please." Elizur emerged from the mouth of the second tunnel and ran up to the platform. "Leviathan accepts the challenge of Behemoth on this condition. The winner will have the right to name any task he wants done, and the loser must carry it out."

The judges looked toward Behemoth. "Do you accept the condition?"

With a harsh grunt of contempt, Behemoth dipped his heavy head in consent.

"He's sure he'll win," Shani said unhappily. "He'll make Baby do some awful thing."

The three judges repeated, "Let the combat commence."

Behemoth rushed straight at Leviathan with his head lowered almost to the ground. His wide-spreading horns, sharp as swords, were thrust forward to gore. Leviathan could not move quickly on land and he did not try to evade the attack. His mighty tail rose and swayed in the air. Shani thought, "Woe to anyone struck by that tail.

In a flash, it did strike Behemoth, with a blow that would have felled a bull elephant. Behemoth staggered slightly. His assault had failed.

At a signal from the judges, a herald tooted on his trumpet and called out, "Round One to Leviathan."

Behemoth moved back and then came at a gallop, and hurled himself at his foe. Leviathan did not have time to bring his tail into action before Behemoth struck with a force that knocked his opponent over on his side. The terrible horns slashed, and Leviathan seemed troubled by them, as much as by mosquito bites. His defenses had been breached.

At a signal from the judges, the other herald tooted on his trumpet and called out, "Round Two to Behemoth."

"How many rounds are there?" Shani asked.

"The judges will decide on two out of three," Zachor said.

"Then this is the one that counts. Oh, I hope . . ."

Behemoth bellowed and dashed around to the other side of Leviathan. Then came a duel in which he fenced with his horns and Leviathan with his tail. Thrust and parry — thrust and parry — neither could touch the other. Suddenly, Behemoth retreated backward toward the mouth of his tunnel.

"He can't be giving up," Shani said. "What is he planning?"

Behemoth began to run toward Leviathan, at a speed amazing for his great weight. Faster and faster he came, and then with all the momentum of his dash he took a bounding leap into the air and came down on Leviathan's back. He stood there and swung his head for a final attack with his terrible horns.

In a swirl of glittering colors, the great tail swung up, stood high in the air for a moment, and swept down. It sent Behemoth into a flipflop in the air before he hit the ground.

44

At a signal from the judges, the first herald tooted on his trumpet and called out, "Round Three to Leviathan."

The judges rose and spoke together. "By two rounds out of three, Leviathan is declared champion."

Both heralds blew two long blasts, as the audience applauded and cheered. At the direction of the heralds, Leviathan and Behemoth took their places facing each other in front of the platform.

The middle judge spoke. "Leviathan, name a task and Behemoth must perform it."

"I'm sure he won't want anything mean," Shani said to the twins. "He wouldn't, would he?"

Leviathan spoke in a voice very like his big brother's, but not so deep.

"Honorable judges, not long ago I came by chance on a small island in the midst of the sea. It's barren and covered with rocks and stones. Some people who were very poor in their old homes came to settle there and try to make a living for themselves. But it's too hard for them, and they'll fail. They have nowhere else to go.

"Therefore," he turned to the glowering Behemoth, "I ask you please to use your tremendous strength to help them. Dig up the rocks and stones, and plow the land for them so they can plant crops."

"You forget one thing, Baby," Behemoth growled. "I cannot swim to that island."

"Don't worry. You can get back on my back, and I'll take you there — a round-trip."

Behemoth nodded grudgingly, and shuffled back to the mouth of his tunnel.

As the audience scattered, the girls made their way to Baby Leviathan. The twins greeted their old friend and introduced Shani. On impulse, she stroked his gleaming tail.

"Your brother was very nice to me," she told him. "Please give him my regards."

"I'll be glad to," he answered politely. "I hope you have a wonderful time in Beyond-Sambatyon."

"I'm having it already."

Zachor turned to Elizur. "You knew Baby was coming, didn't you?"

He nodded. "We've been friends for a few centuries. Recently, Pega-Soos and I happened to meet up with him, and I mentioned Behemoth's challenge."

"How did you get here?" Shani asked Baby. "You can't get over the mountains, can you?" She quickly added, "Of course, I won't ask you to tell anything secret."

"I don't mind telling you, but I'd as soon nobody else knows. There's a passage where the waters of Pan-Oceania flow under the mountains and the River Sambatyon. I came on it by chance once. You can only get through it if you're a pretty good underwater swimmer and no bigger than I am. There's just enough space and air for me to take Behemoth that way."

"You seem to come on a lot of things by chance. Are you another wanderer, like Elizur?"

"Always," he said. "Ever since I really was a baby. I'll never forget the time . . . Well, never mind that. I don't want to bore you with a story."

"That means he's about to tell us a story," Elizur said. "We might as well sit down and be comfortable."

Chapter 8

# Baby Leviathan's Tale

"It was in the days when I was just a little fellow," Baby began. "I wasn't even the size of a whale. I was already very curious about things, but I had never yet been far from home. I had a playground by our coral palace deep in Pan-Oceania, and I wasn't allowed to leave it by myself. Ima and Abba were afraid I would get lost.

"I never meant to be naughty," Baby went on. "I was simply eager to see the wonders of the water-world. Even so, I wouldn't have disobeyed my parents if it weren't for an octopus party. They tempted me. They wriggled by and waved their tentacles to lure me to follow.

"At first I had a grand time. It's very dark down at the bottom of the sea, but there was light from hundreds of electric eels and thousands of glowseaworms. I soon lost the octopus party, but I didn't mind. There was so much to see — manta rays flopping along, and a sea horse race, and long stringy jellyfish and even odder things. If anything looked interesting, I just swam after it.

"By and by, I decided to start for home. Only then did I realized that I had no idea where I was, or which way to turn. Even so, I might have found my way, except that a very peculiar thing happened.

"First, I noticed a strange, harsh smell. Next, I was caught up in such a rush of waters that I could not hold my course. Great undersea waves beat and beat on me, pushing me this way and that. I tried as hard as I could to get out of their way, but they were too strong for me. The waters spun me around until I got dizzy.

"Then I began to hear sounds, like explosions one after the other. The water started to get hot. Guess what it was!"

"A volcano!" Shani answered. "A volcano erupting under the sea!"

"Exactly! I'd heard stories about them, but never been near one. The smell was from sulfur. The heat was from burning-hot lava pouring out of the cone of the volcano.

"I plunged and twisted, and finally I was able to escape the heat and the lava. Can you imagine what happened next?"

Shani thought about that. "Maybe I can. We learned about volcano eruptions and earthquakes in science class. When they happen at sea they can cause a . . . a . . . well, its something with a hard name that I can't exactly remember. It's the worst kind of tidal wave."

"It's called a tsunami," Elizur said.

"I didn't care what it was called," Baby said. "I just wanted to get away from it. I pushed up toward the surface. Things weren't quite as bad there, but the sea was still wild enough to wreck a small ship. This happened long ago, when all ships were small.

"In fact, I was close to a ship that almost was wrecked. When I saw its sails I swam toward it. I meant to ask the captain which sea

I was in. Then tremendous billows began to toss it around like a stick. Men threw things overboard, big clay jugs, chests, bales, all sorts of things. I guess they were trying to lighten the load. It didn't help.

"The ship was just about to break up, or be sucked under. At the last moment, something really frightful happened. The sailors picked up a man and pitched him right over the rail into the sea!

"He sank into the water, but by then I was near enough to make a great spurt of speed and got to him before he went under for the last time. He couldn't manage to climb on my back. There was only one way to save him. I took him in my mouth.

"Then, I was hit by another great wave that turned me over on my side, and . . . and I accidentally swallowed him! He slid right down. He wasn't even hurt. I could hear him calling out, and after a while he seemed to be chanting.

"All at once that terrible tsamu... tsumi... that terrible wave just stopped and the sea was calm as could be. The ship sailed on its way, safe and sound. I never got a chance to talk to the captain.

"Well, then the thought kept coming to me, 'Take the man to land, take the man to land.' Which way was land? I looked all about me, picked a direction on impulse and set off.

"Sometimes I saw land in the distance, but for some reason I always felt it was the wrong place. It was three whole days before I came to a shore that I just felt was the right one. All that time I didn't dare even to drink some water, or I might have drowned the poor man. l was parched and famished before I finally got to a seacoast.

"As carefully as I could, I coughed him up and spit him out. I saw him crawl up onto the land. He never even thanked me. A long, long time later, Elizur told me that the man must have been a prophet named Jonah, who went around telling people he was swallowed by a fish." Baby sounded indignant. "I'm *not* a fish!"

"I was going to ask if it was Jonah," Shani said, "but I didn't want to interrupt your story."

"My story isn't finished," Baby Leviathan told her. "I started out again to find my way home. First I tried to find a meal. Leviathans don't eat any living sea creatures, because they're our subjects. At home we have nice meals of things that grow under water, but I had to make do with bunches of floating seaweed that tasted horrid and left me just as hungry.

"I began to think that if I did not make it home, my family might never know what had become of me." He paused and sighed at the thought of such a fate.

"I just kept going, on what I hoped was the right course. Actually, it wasn't. But along the way, I found something that really whet my curiosity. I came across the wreck of a very old ship, on the bottom of the seabed, almost buried in the sand.

"Of course, I had to stop and inspect it. There were many chests scattered around and leather sacks. Some of them were broken open and pieces of gold and silver had fallen out on the deck, There were a lot of those big clay storage jars that folk used in the olden times, with designs stamped on them and letters written on them. And there were tablets with more letters written on them.

"I could not understand the letters, but I made sure to remember how some of them looked, especially a string of them that I found repeated in many places. Once I drew some of them in wet sand to show to Elizur, and he could read them. He said they were letters from the most ancient Hebrew alphabet, and they spelled out *"Jehoshaphat, King of Judah."*

"I remember him," Elizur said. "He was a good king. Once he built a merchant fleet to sail to Ophir, but it was wrecked. Baby must have come upon one of those lost ships."

"I wanted to see more of the ship, and all the things on it," Baby went on. "But while I was poking around, I suddenly realized that there were big dark shapes near me in the water. Sharks!

"They were drifting slowly and lazily, but heading straight toward me. Young as I was, I was already bigger than the biggest shark, but there were lots and lots of them. And sharks aren't afraid or anyone or anything — not even a Leviathan.

"They formed a circle around me. They swam faster and faster, closing in nearer and nearer. One of them tried to attack me. I hit it a good hard slap with my tail, and it reeled back. Four more came in its place. I had to move fast to knock them away.

"I tried to swim off, but the whole pack came at once, on every side of me. I thought to myself, 'I'm done for.' All I could do was try to be brave, and fight to the end.

"I didn't know that my Ima and Abba and my big brothers and sisters had all been looking for me, fanning out in every direction. My Ima, Queen Leviathan, had come upon some dolphins and asked them to help look for me. Dolphins have their own way of talking, and can hear one another far away. Very quickly, they passed a message throughout the oceans and seas.

"When some of the dolphins spied a pod of whales — who are their cousins, you know — they asked them to join the search. So, when a blue whale, the largest creature in the world after a full-grown Leviathan, saw a tremendous churning of water and heard a lot of commotion, she dived down for a look. The sharks were so bent on their furious attacks on me, they didn't even notice the whale until it was too late. Too late for them, that is.

"'You nasty things,' the whale cried out in a fury. 'All of you together jumping on one baby.' She rushed the whole lot of them. They are so bold, they tried to fight even a blue whale, but the battle was soon over.

"After that, she led me straight home. Along the way, we met up with some of the dolphins who had been looking for me and they came with us. Before long, I was safe back in our palace. You can imagine how thankful my family was to the whale and the dolphins — who have been particularly good friends of the Leviathans ever since."

"But you didn't give up wandering?"

"No. The family knew I never would, so they started taking me on trips with them until I learned my way around. Now I've seen many marvelous things. And everywhere I go, I look for that ship. Someday I'll find it again, and learn whatever secrets it holds."

"I've been seeing some marvelous things myself," Shani told him.

"And more to come," Shamor promised her.

Chapter 9

# A Ride on the PaGaHaP

The next morning, the twins announced to Shani, "We're taking a ride on the PaGaHaP!" The way they pronounced the strange word, Shani could hear the capital letters.

"What is the PaGaHaP?" She wondered if this was another great creature, and they would ride on its back as she had ridden on Duchipat and Leviathan.

"You'll soon find out," Shamor told her.

The three girls went out from the palace and walked until they came to a wide river. They turned to follow along its bank. It could not be the Sambatyon, because there were no leaping rocks.

"What river is this?" Shani asked.

"The PaGaHaP," Zachor answered.

So the PaGaHaP was not a living creature after all.

"I know plenty of rivers from my geography books and my globe, but I never heard of any PaGaHaP."

"You won't find it on your globe," Shamor told her. "It rises in the Garden of Eden and divides into the four rivers that flow out of Eden — the Pishon, the Gihon, the Hidekel and the Prat. Here they flow back together again. So we call it the PaGaHaP."

They came to a pier where a most peculiar boat was hitched. It was built of wooden planks and it was very, very long. An odd sort of house, three stories high, stood on the deck. A rickety gangplank ran down to the pier, and a white-bearded patriarch stood on it as though he were waiting for them. He seemed old beyond counting, but he was spry and peered at them with a lively twinkle.

"Meet a very remarkable sea captain," Zachor said. "This is Noah."

"All aboard!" was his greeting. "We're shipping out."

"Where are you taking us?" Shamor asked.

"Up the River Pishon to Havilah, the land of gold."

Shamor frowned. "Isn't that dangerous?"

"Do you question my seamanship?" Noah demanded, sounding testy.

He steered out into the great river. For all its clumsy construction, the ancient boat made good speed. Shani touched one of the weathered planks and asked, "Is this really the ark? The real ark, I mean?"

"Surely is, little lass. And over many a wave we've been together."

"What was it like with all those animals?"

"It could drive a captain crazy. So many special menus. Do you know that a koala won't touch a thing but eucalyptus leaves? And such squabbling. I had to be a regular referee."

They were at midstream now, and Noah turned the prow eastward. The current carried them along easily.

"She'll do on her own for a while," he said. "I have time for a chantey."

He opened a battered sea chest and took out a musical instrument carved from wood and set with strings. He strummed the strings, and each one twanged with a strange tone. Shani would have loved to try it, but it looked so old and fragile that she did not dare ask to touch it.

"Do you know what 'antediluvian' means?" Noah asked her.

"Not exactly."

"It means 'before-the-Flood,' and that's what this is. My kinsman Jubal made it. In fact, he invented it. The first and original *kinor*.* It's the ancestor of every harp and lute and violin and piano and ukulele and whatever else has strings to make music."

He sat on a bench and strummed some more. At first the notes seemed to clash with one another, but then Shani began to hear a tune in them.

"I had it with me the whole time of the Flood," Noah said. "A little entertainment during a whole year with nowhere to go. Now and then, I'd make up a song. I suppose you'd like to hear one, wouldn't you?"

Without waiting for an answer, he began to sing loudly and off key.

> *It's anchors aweigh,*
> *To a horse's neigh.*
> *A crocodile cries*
> *As the waters rise,*

---

* The Hebrew word *"kinor"* is "stringed instrument" or "violin" in English.

*And a lion roars*
*As the rain still pours.*
*Fox yipping, wolf baying,*
*Shrew scolding, otter playing,*
*Hound-dog yelping, cow mooing,*
*Frog croaking, pigeon cooing,*
*Camel snorting, llama lowing,*
*Walrus huffing, cock crowing,*
*Panda munching, bear grumping,*
*Sloth snoring, beaver thumping,*
*Aardvark scraping, lark singing,*
*Ram bunting, springbok springing,*
*Billy bleating, snake rattling,*
*Yak yakking, squirrel prattling.*

*Snarling panther, calling moose,*
*Yawning hippo, honking goose,*
*Clomping bison, stamping buck,*
*Chirping cricket, quacking duck,*
*Praying mantis, chatting monkey,*
*Squawking parrot, braying donkey,*
*Charging rhino, purring cat,*
*Screeching eagle, squeaking bat.*

*Elephant trumpets, tiger growls,*
*Peccary grunts, coyote howls,*
*Hyena laughs, hummingbird hums,*
*Kangaroo bounds, gorilla drums.*

*A squeal, a crunch, a yowl, a bark —*
*'Twas mighty noisy on the ark!*

Noah finished off with a flourish of chords, and the girls applauded vigorously while he put the *kinor* back in the chest.

"I surely did like the giraffes," he said. "They never made a sound."

The ark was approaching a point where two rivers joined, and Noah went back to his steering. He turned into the Pishon, where the waters were darker and rougher than the bright PaGaHaP. They passed no more meadows blooming with flowers, for the banks here were walled with gnarled and twisted trees that dripped thick screens of mosses.

The current ran strongly, carrying the boat faster and faster onward. They could make out the hazy form of an island in the distance, with sharp rocks piled all along its shore. The ark was rushing straight toward them.

"Will we run into those rocks?" Shani asked nervously.

"Never fear," Noah said, which she did not think was an answer.

"It feels like it's pulling us with a magnet!"

"It is," Shamor said. "The whole of Havilah is a magnetic island. If a boat comes too near, it's pulled in on the rocks. Most of them are wrecked."

"Don't worry," Zachor assured her. "Noah has never had a wreck yet."

Their captain kept a keen watch on the island, while he turned the ark this way and that in a zigzag course. Suddenly, a savage current hit the boat from behind and swept it along. It was driven so hard and so fast by the surge of wildly frothing water that it was quite out of control. One moment it was tossed almost out of the water, and the next moment it was almost sucked under.

The girls cried out in surprise and alarm.

"Hang on tight," Noah yelled to them.

The three clung to one another and to the rail and shrieked as they were drenched in icy spray. They tried to call out, but their voices were lost in the thunderous roar of the raging river. Just when Shani thought they would surely go down, the current rushed past them and the churning river was calm once more. The boat straightened itself and glided along smoothly.

"What was all the hollering for?" Noah snapped. "Didn't you trust me?"

It was not much farther to Havilah, a long narrow island in midstream. Noah drew them into a bay, lowered the gangplank, and led them ashore.

"What's so special about this island?" Shani asked. She was thinking that it should be very special indeed to be worth such a trip.

"Oh, many things. Like the gold. Things you wouldn't expect to be of gold. For instance, there's a crystal tree with apples of pure gold. If we can get to the tree, you can pick one of them to keep."

"Is it hard to get to it? Why?"

"Because it's guarded by the Serpent."

"A serpent? Is it a big one?"

"Not just *a* serpent," Zachor said. *"The* Serpent. The same one that enticed Eve to eat the forbidden fruit in the Garden of Eden. After that, he came here and hid himself away. He grows bigger and bigger, and hates humans more and more."

"Why?"

"Because if Eve and Adam had not let him trick them, he would still be the most beautiful and proud creature in Eden. He blames them that he was driven out of the Garden and made to crawl on his belly. He holds it against all their children forever."

"And if anyone tries to pick one of the golden apples, that reminds him of Eve," Shamor added. "It makes him so furious, he'll gulp them down."

"Where is he now?" Shani looked around cautiously.

"Probably sound asleep in his lair," Noah said. "Maybe."

They went forward, climbing steep and slippery hills. At the very center of Havilah was a single lofty peak. At its top, something glittered in the rays of the sun, and led them on like a beacon. When they had finally scrambled up the slopes, they found the bright object was a great tree of pure crystal. The four of them together could not make a closed circle around its trunk. The leaves on the crystal boughs were of emerald, and scattered among them were apples of gold.

They were so rapt in admiring the beauty of it, that they forgot about the Serpent. They forgot until . . . there he was! His long, long, heavy body slithered out of a dark cave nearby. He moved with amazing speed, and before they realized what he was doing he had swung himself into a ring, head to tail. He became a living wall, with the three girls and Noah standing trapped within it.

He turned a cold, cruel stare from one to another. Then he fixed on Shani.

"You! You're the one who was about to touch an apple. You're the one I'm going to swallow first of all. Then your two pretty chums. The old man looks too tough to digest, I'll just toss him off my mountain."

Shani rallied all her courage, determined not to show how frightened she was.

"Why are you in such a hurry to hurt us?" She tried hard to make her voice firm. "Why do you have to hate everybody?"

"Because everybody hates me," he screeched as though in pain. "Because once I was the loveliest creature in Eden. Now I'm so ugly, I hate anyone to come here and see me."

"You're not ugly."

"I am so. I'm repulsive. I'm disgusting. I disgust you, don't I?"

"No, you don't," Shani insisted. The Serpent sounded so miserable, she began to feel more sorry for him than afraid of him. She remembered Queen Shabbat's mirror, that she always kept carefully buttoned in a deep pocket. She took it out and held it up.

"Look at yourself."

"I won't. I don't want to see me."

"You'll see you have wonderful colors," she promised. "Your scales have more colors than a rainbow."

The Serpent stretched out his neck just far enough to take a peep in the mirror.

"I guess they're not so bad," he admitted.

Zachor joined in. "Such elegant designs."

He took another look in the mirror. "Mmm . . ."

"And you're so graceful and swift," Shamor said admiringly. "You can dart like lightning."

"I guess I'm no slowpoke." He turned his head from side to side, watching himself in the mirror.

"And smart," Noah said. "I wouldn't try to fool you."

"Better not try," the Serpent advised him.

He turned back to Shani. His stare was no longer cold or cruel.

"Why do you want an apple?"

"Because it's so pretty. And as a souvenir of coming here."

"Well, you may have one. I don't mind." He stretched his jaws wide, but only to yawn. "I was taking a nap and you woke me up.

That's why I was just a tiny bit cranky at first. Excuse me, and I'll go finish my snooze for a century or so." With a last admiring glance at himself in the mirror, he slid off into his lair.

Shani selected an apple. Then the little band started down the road back to shore and the ark.

"The poor thing was so unhappy for so long," Shani said sadly.

"He won't be any more, thanks to you," Shamor said.

&a &a &a

On the sail back down the Pishon, Noah managed to avoid the wild waters and before long they were once more on the calm waters of the PaGaHaP. The current had changed, and carried them homeward with little need for steering. Noah drew on a rope that had been dangling over the side of the ark, pulled up a leather bottle, uncorked it and took a deep swallow.

"Nothing like a sip of wine after a hard trip," he said. "I make it myself, so I know it's good. The water keeps it cool."

"He's been having those sips ever since the Flood," Shamor whispered.

Noah took some more swallows and then some deeper gulps. Then he slumped down on his bench and fell sound asleep. The twins went off for a stroll around the decks, but Shani chose to stay leaning on the rail, watching flecks of sunlight dancing on the river.

When she heard cawing and cooing, she looked up and saw two birds circle the ark and settle down to perch on the rail. She recognized them easily.

The dove, puffing up, said smugly, "Don't you know the Song of Songs? The young man calls his sweetheart *O, my dove* — not *O, my raven.*"

The raven, wings flapping, retorted, "And she admires him because his hair is black as a raven, not gray as a dove."

The dove puffed up even more. "Romeo says Juliet is a snowy dove, not a sooty raven."

The raven flapped even harder. "Edgar Allen Poe wrote his famous poem about a raven, not a dove."

"Don't they ever get tired of it?" Shani wondered, as she too was dozing off. She woke up when the ark bumped into the pier from which they had embarked. The two birds had gone.

Chapter 10

# A Look Into the Past

Late that afternoon, Shani sat with the twins on the verandah at the back of the palace. They lounged on swinging seats and chatted.

"We have a while yet before dinner," Zachor said. "We have time to go to the Wax Figure Theater. It's near by."

The theater was a round building set in the palace gardens. There was a stage covered by curtains, and rows of chairs facing it. The rest of the circular wall had many miniature stages set in into it, with painted scenery and furnishings that would have fit Shani's old dollhouse. On each stage there were little wax figures, dressed in costumes perfect to the last tiny bead or buckle.

Shani ran from one scene to another. Some seemed familiar from stories she had read or heard. She wanted to linger at each one, and at the same time was eager to get on to the next.

One of the figures she knew instantly, and not just from a story. There was her friend Elijah the Prophet, looking just as he had when he came to visit her. The setting was a on a mountain, under a cloudless and hot-looking sky. Far below, was the sea. Elijah stood at the center, beside a stone altar.

Throngs of people were crowded around, watching him. She could tell from their costumes that this was in biblical times. One band of men stood apart from the others, huddled together. They had cruel faces, and they looked frightened.

"I know it! I know it!" Shani cried in excitement. "This is the story I read about him."

She turned to the twins and went on eagerly. "It happened that time long ago, when there was no rain for so long. That was when the people followed the prophets of a pagan god called Baal. Elijah challenged those prophets to a contest, on Mount Carmel, in the Land of Israel. I guess this is supposed to be Mount Carmel."

"Yes," Zachor said. "Go on."

"Elijah won the contest, and the people would not follow the pagan prophets any more. After that, it began to rain."

She broke off, a little embarrassed. "Of course, I don't have to tell you all this. You both know all about it already."

"Yes, but we like to hear you tell it." Shamor said.

"And just think," Shani added. "Because I read that story, I wished that Elijah would help us. And that is why I am here with you now in Beyond-Sambatyon."

Some of the other scenes she could recognize, and some she could not. One of those was a man wearing a caftan and turban sat at a table, absorbed in something he was writing on parchment.

"He looks so wise. Who is he?"

"He should look wise," Zachor said. "That's the Rambam —
Rabbi Moses Maimonides, the great scholar. When you are older,
you'll read the book you see him writing there."

In another scene there were sailing ships crowded together in
a river. Many men, women and children, carrying boxes and
sacks, were boarding the ships. All looked sad and some were
weeping.

"Those Jews are being driven out of their homes in Spain by cruel
King Ferdinand and Queen Isabella," Shamor told her.

Many scenes farther along, was a forest landscape. A young man
who seemed to be a soldier was lying on the ground, with other men
gathered around him. They looked very mournful.

"Those are clothes from the time of the American Revolution,"
Shani said. "Who is that young man? Is he wounded? Is he dying?"

"Yes. Sad to say, he is dying," Shamor told her. "His name is
Francis Salvador. He was a Jew from England who settled in the
American colony of South Carolina. When the American Revolution
started, he became a leader in the fight for liberty. He was mortally
wounded in battle."

Farther on, they came to a striking, dignified man with a full
beard. He was standing on a platform, addressing an audience.

"There's a picture of him in our classroom. Theodor Herzl."

When they had looked at all the little stages, Shamor said, "Now
comes the theater part. Each of these scenes is part of a story. Which
one do you want to see acted out?"

"All of them."

"We have time for only one."

Shani looked around and made her choice. "I'm sure I know who
this is. Let's see if I'm right."

They took seats, and the light began to dim until the theater was in darkness. Then the curtains opened to show the large stage lit as though by sunshine pouring through the window painted on the backdrop. The scene was exactly like the miniature, except that the wax figures and the setting were life-size.

It was a room with stone walls and colorful hangings. There were many men there, clad in long fringed tunics. At the center, a man was seated on a chair of carved wood decorated with ivory. He was very handsome, with red-gold hair waving around his headband.

Shani had supposed the figures would work like marionettes, and was surprised when they began to move very naturally.

"What's happening?" she whispered.

"You don't have to whisper," Zachor told her. "They're just models in wax. The events they're acting out happened 3,000 years ago."

"They speak in ancient Hebrew," Shamor added. "We've set the voices to come on in English translation."

One of the group of men stepped forth and spoke to the man seated at the center of the stage.

"Hear us, O, David. We are the Chief Elders of all the Tribes of Israel. I am of the Tribe of Issachar, and have been chosen to speak for us all."

The other men nodded their heads in agreement. The Elder of Issachar went on.

"We have come here to your capital city of Hebron to say this to you. Even in the days of King Saul, you led the men of Israel. Seven years you have reigned as King of Judah. The time has come for you to be King of All Israel."

Again the others nodded their agreement.

"Make a covenant with us, that you will rule justly and keep the Law, and every tribe will follow you."

David rose from his chair and answered in a beautiful, musical voice. "I vow to you, I shall rule justly and defend Israel from its enemies."

For the next few seconds the stage was dark, then the light rose again. The scene was the same, and David was seated in his chair. This time, he wore a crown. The tribal Elders were there, and now there were also other men in the scene, some of them soldiers.

David spoke. "Now that all Israel is one nation, and I have been crowned as its King, we must have one, special city to be the heart of our whole land and of all our tribes together."

"Can you tell us where it shall be, my lord King?" The question came from a powerfully built, grim-faced man.

"I can, Joab. It shall be Jerusalem. It is the ideal place for our royal city."

Another man, who looked much like Joab but was even taller and huskier, spoke.

"The King of the Jebusites holds Jerusalem. Its fortress of Zion is atop a steep hill and very strong. My brother Joab is a great warrior, and you are fortunate to have him for your commander, but he cannot walk through walls."

"I do not think, Abishai, that it is walls your brother will walk through." David turned to Joab and said with a smile. "Do you guess what I am thinking?"

Joab, too, smiled a little as he gave a quick nod. "The Jebusites boast that we cannot touch them. It is not good to be boastful."

David stood, looked about at his men, and said, "Whoever is the first to enter Jerusalem will be highest-ranking general of the Kingdom of Israel."

The lights went out. Shani waited impatiently for the next scene to begin.

It was night, but the stage was not entirely dark. Rays of moonlight sparkled on a spring of water rushing from a rocky cleft. More light came from a flaming torch held by a youth who stood beside Joab and Abishai.

Joab whispered, "Bring the torch closer, Benaiah. We must find the opening quickly."

The two men and the boy searched among the boulders. Benaiah said excitedly but in a low voice, "Here it is. The mouth of the tunnel."

"The Jebusites didn't even set a guard here. Not one man in their watchtower." Abishai said scornfully. "They're inviting us in."

"Maybe they never guessed we would think of this way under the walls."

Joab gave a sharp birdlike whistle, and several men with spears and swords came out of the shadows.

"The Jebusites made this tunnel to bring water into Jerusalem," Joab told them. "Now it will bring us in. When we are in the city, we will open the gates. David waits to enter with his other mighty men of valor. I will go first, and become chief commander over all the host of Israel. Those who dare to follow me will be officers and have rewards from the King. Who is coming?"

"I am!" Benaiah answered at once.

"You?" Abishai said. "You're only a boy, too young to be a fighting man."

"Let him come," Joab ruled. "Keep behind me, lad. If you learn enough from me, you may be the King's general after me. But not for many years yet," he added with a harsh chuckle.

"Was he?" Shani asked.

"Yes," Shamor said, "In the days of his friend King Solomon."

Joab went into the opening in the rock. Abishai and Benaiah and the others came close after him. This scene faded and was quickly replaced by one that showed the inside of the tunnel. A stream ran through it, and the men were standing in the water.

Joab pointed ahead of them. "It will be a tough climb, but we are going to do it. Stay beside me with the torch, boy, and we'll lead the way."

The men disappeared into the darkness, and the scene faded again. This time it was followed by a scene of a stone chamber with a wide round opening in the floor. There were five men there, all in the gear of soldiers. Four were asleep on mats on the floor, their weapons dropped carelessly beside them. The fifth was awake, busy drinking from a beer jug. He did not notice when Joab peered over the edge of the hole in the floor.

"Ooh, I hope they don't wake up." Shani spoke in a whisper, though she knew she did not have to.

"Silly," Zachor said. "Didn't I tell you it was all over 3,000 years ago?"

"Yes, I know, but I worry anyway. It seems so real."

Joab glanced back into the tunnel, and touched his lips as a signal for silence. Then he sprang like a leopard into the guardroom. Abishai was right behind him. Before the astonished sentry could move or cry out, Abishai seized him and held him fast. The men who had followed him out of the shaft did the same with the other four Jebusites, who were dazed at being startled out of their deep sleep.

"Put those four into the tunnel," Joab ordered. "Cover the opening with that stone lid there. If they shout, nobody will hear them."

He turned to the fifth guard, still held by Abishai. "Lead us to the gateway, and you'll have a bag of silver. Try to trick us, and you'll be sorry."

The back wall of the chamber dissolved and the gateway of Jerusalem appeared. A bright full moon shone upon it. On either side of the gates were high walls. Before the gateway was an open space with stone benches, where several guards were lolling. Only one stood sentry by the gate.

When he saw the men coming, he said, "Ah, the relief guard. You've come early." Then he saw his mistake, but by that time the powerful Abishai had him in his grip. The other guards were just as quickly overpowered.

"Open the gate," Joab commanded, and several of his men leaped to the task. As they struggled with the heavy bronze bolts, Joab drew a shofar from his belt and blew a long quivering blast. From outside the wall came an answering blast. The gates were flung wide open, and David stood on the threshold of the city. Behind him pressed his warriors. With a great thunder of battle cries they poured through the gateway and into Jerusalem.

As the dawn rose, officers and soldiers and all of the Elders gathered around the King.

The Elder of Issachar proclaimed, "From now on, this hill where we stand shall be known as the City of David."

The King said, "And the Children of Israel shall make this a holy city, and built a Temple here."

The early morning sun cast a glow of rosy gold over the scene, as the curtains closed on the stage.

The lights came back on in the theater. Shani, still caught up in the deeds she had seen enacted, was silent. She was trying to make sure she would remember every detail to report when she got back to school.

*Chapter 11*

# Finding the Lost Tribes

The next morning, Shani asked "What's our adventure today?" Zachor smiled as though she had a secret, and then blurted it out. "A visit to the Lost Tribes of Israel."

"And we have to start out soon," Shamor said. "Their city of Shalem is a long way off."

"Too far to walk," Zachor added. "We'll ride part way."

They took seats in what would have been a pony-cart, except that it was drawn by a zebra who took them along at a brisk trot.

"While we're riding, tell me about the Lost Tribes," Shani said. "I've heard of them, but I don't know much about them."

"It's an ancient story, and a very sad one," Zachor began. "The Twelve Tribes of Israel were united in one kingdom in the time of Saul and David and Solomon. After that, the tribes split up, into the Kingdom of Judah in the south of the Land, and the Kingdom of Israel in the north."

Shamor took up the tale. "Alas, more than 2,700 years ago, a King of Assyria came with his mighty forces and conquered the Northern Kingdom. He carried off many of its people into exile in faraway places and they never came back. So they are called the Lost Tribes."

"That is, the world thinks they're lost," Zachor went on. "But many of their descendants are tucked away here in a corner of Beyond-Sambatyon, waiting until the time comes for them to return to the Land of their fathers."

They were now on a road that turned up a steep hill. As they climbed, they could hear a sound of rushing waters, that soon grew to a roar. When they rolled out onto flat ground, they were on a ledge half-way up a stone cliff. A cascade of foaming water, spangled by the sun, poured over the top of the cliff and tumbled down its face into a swift-running stream far below. Arched over the cliff and the waterfall was the most splendid rainbow that Shani had ever seen or imagined. Every shade of color glowed in it — deep red and royal purple, sparkling blue and brilliant green, sunny yellow and burning orange. She gasped at the sight.

"Look closely," Shamor told her.

Shani gazed intently at the rainbow, and little by little she made out something. Along the arc there were Hebrew letters in blazing gold. With the help of the twins, she read these words: *The Gate of Promise — The Eternal Covenant of God and Israel.*

Shani felt such wonder that she spoke in a whisper. "What does it mean?"

"This is the rainbow that appeared after the Flood," Shamor told her.

Shani would have liked to linger longer, but they had to go on with the journey. They unhitched the zebra to graze and rest until they returned. Then they walked along the broad ridge, passing between the wall of rock and the screen of falling water. They were sprinkled by the spray, but they did not mind that one bit. Halfway across, they came to an opening in the face of the cliff and the twins turned toward it.

"Is it a cave?" Shani asked. "It's dark. Do we have to go in?"

"It's not really a cave," Shamor said. "It's a passageway to the other side of the cliff, and the Kingdom of the Lost Tribes."

With that encouragement, Shani followed her friends through the opening and into a tunnel. With a start, she saw a very strange kind of creature whose long, slithery body was coiled up across the entrance, as though keeping guard on it. She drew back from it so quickly that she stumbled.

Before she could ask a question, Zachor introduced the creature. "This is the shamir. It can cut right through the hardest stone. There is a legend that Moses used it to engrave the names of the Twelve Tribes of Israel on the gems worn by the High Priest."

"Also," Shamor added, "it solved King Solomon's problem in building the Temple in Jerusalem. Metal is used to make weapons of war, so it could not be used in the tools to build the Temple. So how could the huge stones be cut and shaped?"

"By the shamir?"

"Yes. Ashmodai had it then. He was very jealous of it."

Shani remembered her meeting with Ashmodai. She would not care to meet him again.

"It took all Solomon's wit to get the shamir away from Ashmodai. That's a story for another day," Zachor said.

"It also cut this passage," Shamor said. "It's the only way to reach the Lost Tribes. I don't think the shamir would let any enemy get by."

"You don't have to be afraid of it," Zachor assured her. "It knows us well."

Indeed, the shamir gave them no trouble. It did not even stir as they passed. Still, Shani kept as far away from it as she could. The tunnel was dim and, it seemed to her, spooky. The only sounds were the echo of their steps and the few low words they exchanged now and then. Hundreds of fireflies swarmed before them, glowing to show the girls their road.

It was a dull walk and a long one until at last there was a glimmer of daylight ahead. Forgetting that they were weary, the girls ran toward it. Soon the gloomy passage was behind them, and they stood out in the sunshine in the country of the Lost Tribes of Israel. Shani looked about and smiled because the scenery was so pretty.

The quiet was broken by a sound as though several shofars were blowing *teruah* all together.

"It's a greeting for us," Zachor told Shani.

The blast was followed by a rapid beat of hoofs, and three horsemen appeared on the crest of a hill. Each of them had red hair and a red beard, and they twirled swords in the air above their heads as they galloped down toward the newcomers. Shani was a bit startled at this wild display, but the twins hailed the riders like old friends. They reined in their spirited steeds and came to a halt beside the girls.

"This is Shani," Shamor told them. "She is our guest from the outside, and we have brought her to visit you."

"You are very welcome," one of them said. "This is Asher, this is Gad, and I am Dan. We will take you to our King."

He helped Shani to mount his horse and set her front of him. She now felt perfectly comfortable and secure. The other two took the twins up, and off they rode at a canter.

Before long, they came to the outskirts of a city. Slowing down to a walk, they followed a road to a fine large building with walls of white alabaster and gates of black onyx. Around the walls and over the gates, verses of Torah were inscribed in gilded letters.

They entered an inner courtyard, where palm trees stood with their fronds swaying in a soft breeze. Waters splashed in a marble fountain. A man sat on a throne beneath a canopy. He had a kindly look, and his hair and beard were not red but pure white. When they entered his court, he rang a bell with a silvery tone. From other courts and rooms many more bells answered, each with a different ring. They all blended together into a charming harmony.

He saw Shani's enjoyment and was obviously pleased. "We learned this kind of music from the Levites of old," he told her. "Thus we welcome guests."

After the chiming chorus faded away, he gave one more tinkle with his own bell. Six girls answered this summons, and brought stools and small tables and trays laden with fruits and cakes and goblets of chilled juices. While the travelers sat and rested and ate, their host became acquainted with the visitor.

"I am Joseph," he began, "King of the Lost Tribes."

"I'm honored to meet Your Majesty," Shani answered politely. She thought perhaps she ought to stand up and curtsey, but feared she might knock over or spill something. So she just said, "I am Shani from America, and I am very glad to be here."

"It is a deep secret that we live in this place. Only a select few know it. Of course, anyone Shamor and Zachor bring to us must be a friend. But how do you come to be in Beyond-Sambatyon?"

Shani told her long story from the very beginning, and the King listened with great interest. At the end, he said, "So, you are one of the Israelites of the Tribes of Judah and Benjamin who live outside of Beyond-Sambatyon."

"Yes. There are many of us."

King Joseph said sadly, "What a pity that we are not all united as we once were. It was a dreadful mistake when the Tribes of Israel did not all stay together."

"But now we have an independent State of Israel," Shani said. "I've been there twice. My mother's brother went to live there."

His face brightened with happiness. "We have learned of it. In all the twenty-seven centuries we have been here, no news from the outside world has given us such joy as that."

"Jews from all over the world are going back to Israel. Can't you all go too?"

He sighed and shook his head. "Not yet. It is part of our special destiny, that would be hard for you to understand. Some day, there will be a blast of the Great Shofar for us. That will be our signal, and we too will go home to our ancient Land. But in the meantime, we must wait."

He withdrew into thought for a while. Then he looked up and smiled and his voice took on a merry note.

"We have talked of serious things. Now it is time for some entertainment."

He rang twice on his bell and two young men appeared.

"These are my sons, Manasseh and Ephraim," he presented them. "They will be your hosts."

They bowed courteously and ushered the girls into another and much larger courtyard, that had a stage at one end and curtains behind the platform. They settled themselves on benches with soft cushions, and a number of people from other parts of the palace came to join them.

The curtains opened and men in long linen robes filed out onto the stage. Each of them carried a musical instrument — lyre or harp, flute or trumpet or cymbals. One of them acted as the conductor, and Ephraim told Shani that he was Korah, who had been Chief Musician in the Temple of Jerusalem.

First, this orchestra played alone, lovely and haunting music. Then the curtains parted again and a choir appeared, girls wearing gowns of pale green and silver ribbons in their red hair. Shani thought a chorus of angels could not sing more sweetly.

Next came a troupe of women with timbrels. The last to enter was taller than the others, very straight and proud, with a strong, handsome face.

"Who is she?" Shani whispered.

"Guess," Manasseh whispered back.

"Is it . . . Could it possibly be . . . Miriam?"

"A good guess."

The musicians played, the choir sang, and Miriam led the women in dance. They tapped on their timbrels as they whirled and swooped, skirts and veils of many colors billowing around them.

Shani was most reluctant to agree when the twins said, "It's time to start back."

When they took their farewell of King Joseph, he gave Shani a gold chain with a pendant in the form of a tiny gold palm tree.

"The palm tree is an emblem of the Land of Israel, and it also grows here in the Land of Beyond-Sambatyon," he told her. "When you wear this, it will remind you of both."

Dan and Asher and Gad lifted them onto the horses and took them as far as the opening in the wall of the great rock cliff. As the girls entered the dark passage, they waved to the riders, who returned the salute. The two parties waved back and forth until they could no longer see one another.

&#10078; &#10078; &#10078;

When they came back to the place where they had left the zebra and the pony-cart, Shamor said "We've time for a short stop in Toyville. It's not far from here."

"We wouldn't want you to miss it," Zachor added.

When Shani saw Toyville, she was glad she had not missed it. The place was under a great round dome of clear crystal, and was filled with toys on shelves, on tables and on rugs spread over the ground. There were dolls of many kinds, each in a different costume. There were rocking-horses, scooters, tricycles and bicycles. Model trains whizzed along their tracks, model boats sailed on a little pond, and painted kites fluttered overhead. There were marbles in glowing colored glass, pinwheels dazzlingly bright and swift, and tops spinning all over the place. There were beautifully made boards and pieces for playing all the games she knew and others she did not know.

'When the twins invited Shani to pick out a gift for herself, it was not easy to make a choice. Then she saw a doll dressed in a costume that reminded her of the pictures in her book of Bible stories. Her eyes were sparkling rubies. She looked so alive, she seemed almost about to speak. Of course, Shani was too old to play with dolls, but even grown-ups sometimes collect rare and special dolls. Surely this one was rare and special enough to collect.

By the time they got back to the palace, Shani was so weary she could barely stay awake long enough to have supper with the twins. Then she went to her room and to sleep, clasping the doll with the ruby eyes.

*Chapter 12*

# *The Witch of En-dor*

Shani was walking down a strange road. It was neither day nor night. Neither sun nor star could be seen in the sky. A crescent moon, pale and dull in a haze of cloud, hung low on the horizon. There was not a sound to be heard but her own lonely steps. It was scary, but she kept on her way. There was something important she must do, but she could not remember what it was.

She pushed her way through a tangle of thick foliage into a bare clearing. Opposite her was the mouth of a cave. She could make out a flickering circle of candles. They gave off a strange heavy scent that made her drowsy.

"Am I awake or asleep?" she wondered.

Standing in the center of the clearing was a stone statue that towered over her. It was a woman who wore a high crown and held a spear. Her face was hard and stern, the eyes set with large rubies that seemed to glare at Shani.

84

A grating voice called from the depths of the cave. "Come closer, girl, so I can see you better."

It was a commanding voice, and Shani was drawn toward it against her will. When she began to make things out in the semi-darkness, she saw an old woman sitting on a stool. Her gray hair was long and wild and tangled. Strings of gold and silver coins dangled from her scrawny neck.

Beside her a big black bird was chained to a perch, beating its wings furiously. On the other side of the old woman, a snake lay on a cushion, its body coiled round and round and round. It raised its head, stretched wide its jaws and flicked its scarlet forked tongue. Shani was very frightened and started to back out of the cave.

"Don't go," the woman ordered. "It won't strike unless I tell it to. Come closer."

Shani felt she must obey.

"Do you know whose cave you are in, girl?"

Shani shook her head.

"You ought to know me," the hag cackled. "I'm famous. I'm the Witch of En-dor."

Shani had indeed read a story about her. She did not dare ask what the witch was doing here in Beyond-Sambatyon.

Instead, she said, "I know about you, ma'am. I know how poor King Saul came to you for help. You called up the ghost of Samuel. He told Saul that he and his sons would die in battle with the Philistines. But he didn't give up. He fought anyway."

"Hah. You call him poor King Saul," she snarled. "You think he was brave, do you? He was a wicked man because he tried to chase all witches out of his kingdom. But I took revenge on him. That ghost of Samuel was a big fake. I was the one who told Saul his fate, and sent him away with no hope left."

She gave another cackling laugh. The bird beat its wings even harder and gave a raucous caw. The snake again flicked its scarlet forked tongue and hissed.

Shani ran out of the cave, across the clearing and into the bushes. The blazing ruby eyes of the statue seemed to follow her.

She was relieved to be away from the dreadful cave, and back in the fresh air, and even more relieved to find that she was no longer alone. Machshavah and Ma'aseh, whom she had met at the Queen's palace, were coming down the path toward her.

"Whatever are you doing way out here at this hour?" Machshavah asked.

"I don't know," Shani admitted.

"This is a dangerous place to be," Ma'aseh warned.

"I know," she said, with a shudder. She told them about the cave and the witch, the statue, the black bird and the snake.

Then she asked, "What are you two doing here?"

"We have very serious business," Ma'aseh said. He did not tell her what it might be.

"Stay near us," Machshavah said. "Be very quiet."

They came up to the clearing and peered in through the screen of leaves. In the dim light they saw the witch performing a jerky, hobbling dance around the statue, croaking a song.

> *I trick and fake,*
> *For badness sake.*
> *I scheme and plot,*
> *To fill my pot.*

*I move by stealth,*
*To take their wealth.*
*I make them sad,*
*That makes me glad.*
*I sneer and jeer,*
*For my good cheer.*
*I spread a blight,*
*That's my delight.*
*I am a witch,*
*I'll never switch.*

With a harsh laugh, she returned to her cave. Shani and the two men stayed hidden. Soon it grew just light enough for them to see an elderly couple enter the clearing. The man carried a basket filled with fruits and vegetables. The woman also carried a basket, piled with loaves of bread. They placed the baskets on the ground in front of the statue, bowed to it, and left without a word. Nobody else came into the clearing, but somehow the baskets quickly disappeared.

They waited a while. Another and younger couple appeared. They brought a long cloak of velvet. Shani heard the man say, "She demands too much. We can't go on bringing her rich gifts every month."

"Hush," the woman said fearfully. "She's a goddess. She knows everything. She'll punish us if we don't obey."

"Nonsense. Someone is plain robbing us."

The man had dared to speak out loud. At once, sparks flashed from the rubies. Two rough-looking men ran from the cave, grabbed him and dragged him inside. The woman stood terrified.

"Begone from this sacred place," a voice boomed from the statue. "Begone, or you will be struck by lightning." The woman fled in panic. She vanished down a path, wailing and crying.

Machshavah whispered to Ma'aseh, "We'll wait for half an hour. By then it will be pitch dark. Then we can go at our work without being seen."

"No," Shani protested. "In half an hour it will be sunrise." She looked up at the sky for the first streaks of dawn, but it had gone from dark blue to almost black. It was so confusing . . .

At last the crescent moon set. The only light came from the ring of candles still burning around the idol.

Ma'aseh whispered, "Now."

"You wait for us here," Machshavah told Shani.

The two men moved slowly across the clearing. Shani decided that as much as she feared the cave, she would rather be with them than alone in the dark, so she went along.

When the three came to the mouth of the cave they peeked inside, and found it empty. The men nodded to one another and went back to the statue. Shani watched curiously as they probed the stone figure. Ma'aseh even rolled over a large rock and climbed upon it to reach the head. While he was up there, Machshavah found what they were seeking. At the back of the giantess was a hidden spring. When he pressed it, a panel sprang open. The statue was hollow.

Ma'aseh stepped into the cavity. Machshavah and Shani stayed outside watching him. A trapdoor was set into the base. When he lifted it, they saw a narrow flight of steps almost as steep as a ladder. The men took candles from the ring of lights and guarding them carefully made their way slowly down the steps.

Shani felt sure they were on the trail of an exciting secret. She did not want to miss it, and she did not want to stay by herself in the clearing where the witch might come back at any moment. She took a candle and went after them.

At the bottom of the steps they came to a door bolted on the outside. They lifted the bolt and opened the door a crack. Within, they found a small chamber dug out of the earth. No enemy lurked there. The only occupant was the man who had been dragged off to the cave, happy indeed to be set free.

A passageway ran past the door and onward under the ground. It was low and narrow, so Ma'aseh, who was much thinner than Machshavah, went on alone. He soon returned and reported, "It's just as we thought. This passage leads through the cave to the witch's house."

Machshavah explained to Shani, "We have long suspected that there was some trickery going on here. We were right."

Shani remembered how the witch had confessed to deceiving King Saul. "How did she fool people?" she asked.

"Through the statue. It was always her own voice speaking. She frightened folk into thinking it had magical powers, so they brought all kinds of gifts to appease it."

"She won't play that game anymore," Ma'aseh said. "She can't, once everybody knows the truth."

"And we'll make her give back everything she took," Machshavah added.

The man they had rescued now told them, "I must go find my poor wife and tell her the good news." With many thanks to them, he went off.

Machshavah pointed up to the glittering rubies.

"The witch must have used lighted candles inside there to make them blaze and frighten people still more."

"And to give signals to her henchmen, too," Ma'aseh guessed.

Shani had been sitting listening to all this. It seemed to her that the rubies were growing even larger and still shooting sparks toward her. Even knowing how the witch had faked it all, she was so frightened that she began to cry. She felt the ground quiver beneath her, and felt herself quiver too . . .

ও ও ও

She heard familiar voices, but they seemed to be far away.

"Shani, Shani, wake up."

Her room was full of early morning light. Shamor and Zachor stood by her bed and were gently shaking her.

"You were having a bad dream," Shamor said.

"We were in our own rooms and could hear you crying," Zachor told her.

Shani sat up, looked around the room she now knew so well, and at her friends.

"Where is the Witch of En-dor?" she asked, bewildered.

"Only in your dream," Shamor said.

"And the terrible idol with the ruby eyes?"

They gestured toward her pillow. There beside her was the doll with the ruby eyes.

Chapter 13

# Elizur Rides Again

After breakfast, the girls were sitting on the verandah when they heard Elizur's voice calling to them. He was riding on Pega-Soos, who was floating in the air just above the trees. They came down lower, and Elizur slid to the ground.

"We hurried home to be sure to see Shani before she leaves."

"You promised to tell me another story from your adventures," she reminded him.

"And so I will. I've had so many of them, I don't know where to start. What kind of story would you like to hear?"

"One about the Land of Israel in the olden times," she said promptly. "And of course with Pega-Soos in it."

"I'll tell you about one that happened more than 2,000 years ago.

It was in the days when Antiochus, a Greek who was King of Syria, ruled over Judea and all the Land of Israel. I guess you re-member him from the story of Hanukkah.

"He wanted all his subjects to worship pagan idols. He tried to force our people to give up Judaism. Many who remained faithful were cruelly punished or even murdered. In those terrible times, the family we call the Maccabees rose up to fight for our Land and our liberty.

"Judah Maccabee was our commander, and his four brothers were all by his side. His spirit was so great that he inspired his men to do battle even when we were very few and the enemy very many. Everywhere that Jews were oppressed, he came to their rescue.

"The King was furious that the Jews dared to defy him. He sent one general after another to crush us. Judah and his brothers led us from victory to victory. Each time the King's force was defeated, he sent another and even larger one. We had to fight one battle after another. We could never let down our guard.

"There was a time when two generals, named Nicanor and Gorgias, attacked Judea with 40,000 men and 7,000 warhorses. The King ordered them not just to defeat the rebels, but to enslave or kill every Jew and destroy Jerusalem. He meant to divide up the Land of Israel among strangers.

"Judah and his men knew that they must win, or our people and our country would be destroyed. He had to make us stronger and better trained. He also had to know what the enemy was planning, so he sent out scouts to learn all they could and report to him. I was one of those scouts.

"Nicanor and Gorgias had set up their camp on the plain at Emmaus, near the roads that lead into the Judean hills. Emmaus was a beautiful town, people came to bathe in the hot springs. But I was not there for luxury. I was pretending to be a deaf-mute slave boy. That way, nobody paid any heed to me, and I could wander around the camp and watch and listen.

"The generals knew that the Maccabees had only about 3,000 men and not even enough weapons for them. They were so sure of victory, that Nicanor invited slave-traders to come and buy the prisoners he expected to capture. They came, bringing gold and silver to pay him, and chains to bind the slaves.

"One day, I noticed the two generals go into a tent alone, and not let anyone else come in. I guessed this meant they had very important secrets to talk about. I grabbed up a jug of wine, and went into the tent. They thought I could not hear a word they said, so they let me stay and pour out wine for them.

"What they said made me shiver. They knew that Judah had his own camp at Mizpeh, a few hours march from Emmaus. That very night, Gorgias was going to take 5,000 men and 1,000 warhorses through the hills in the dark, for a surprise attack. He was sure that would be the end of the Maccabees, and the Jews would be crushed.

"I had to keep my wits about me and get this news to Judah in time. My precious Pega-Soos was waiting for me in a cave in the nearby hills. I had to get to him . . .

"I left the tent, trying not to seem in a rush. When Gorgias turned and stared at me, I made gestures to show I was going to get more wine. Outside the tent, I had to hold myself back from running, and stroll away without attracting attention. When a sentry stopped me, I just acted silly and he decided I was a harmless fool and let me pass.

"But someone must have been suspicious. Maybe Gorgias wondered why I had not come back with the wine. I heard shouts, 'Go after that boy! Bring him back!' I was careless and made the mistake of looking behind me. That let slip that I could hear. The soldiers must have guessed that I had been faking, and why.

"I started to run as fast as I could. Luckily, I had a good head start. They shot arrows and spears at me, and some came pretty close. One ripped my tunic and cut me, though not badly.

"Men started after me on horseback, and of course I had no chance of outrunning them. But by that time I was into the hills that I knew so well. I dodged from spot to spot and hid behind boulders and bushes. Some of them galloped past without seeing me crouched behind an old stone wall.

"I finally reached the cave, exhausted and out of breath. I threw myself on Pega-Soos' back and gasped out to him that we must fly straight to Mizpeh. In minutes we were in Judah's camp. In more minutes, Judah had a plan."

Elizur picked up a twig from the ground and scratched some circles and lines in the earth. "Here is Mizpeh," he pointed to one circle, "and here is Emmaus, about fifteen miles away. It is the dark of night now. Judah rallies his 3,000 men with brave words — he was always wonderful at doing that — and marches them out of Mizpeh. Where do you think he was going?"

"To Jerusalem?" Shani took a guess.

"No. The enemy was still holding Jerusalem then."

"Someplace safe, away from the enemy?"

Elizur laughed. "Not Judah! He was too bold for that. He marched them along this line . . ." he traced it out, "straight to Emmaus. Right to the enemy camp. Only 3,000 of them, to attack the 35,000 men and 6,000 horses there with Nicanor.

"Three of his four brothers — Johanan, Jonathan and Simon — went with him. His brother Eleazar . . . I'll come to him in a minute.

"Gorgias with his 5,000 men and 1,000 horses were marching in the other direction, heading for Mizpeh. He expected a quick and easy victory. Our men had left campfires alight so Gorgias would think they were still there and did not expect an attack. He came charging into the camp . . . and found it empty!

"He guessed Judah must have been warned he was coming. But he believed that the Maccabees were frightened of him and had run away to hide. He set right out to find them.

"Now, here is something that never got into the history books, so just try to imagine it. Suppose that Judah's brother Eleazar did not march with him to Emmaus. Suppose that instead he took a small band of men to act as decoys.

"Eleazar could let Gorgias get a glimpse of his band and start after them. Then they could disappear into the hills. When Gorgias had gone in the wrong direction for a while, they could reappear behind him and lead him off on another wild-goose chase. Can you guess why?"

"I think so," Shani said. "It would keep Gorgias out of the way, so Judah would not have to fight all his soldiers too."

"Smart girl. In the meantime, Judah led his men down from the hills. It was already daybreak when they reached Nicanor's base at Emmaus, too late to make a surprise attack in the dark.

"Nicanor saw how small Judah's force was. He commanded his warriors to march out onto the plain and attack. Our men were out-numbered by more than ten to one, but Judah cried out to them in words that gave them heart and courage.

"They blew their trumpets and advanced. Nicanor's troops fell into a panic and fled across the plain to escape to the coast. They abandoned their camp, and Judah had it set on fire."

"Were you there with Judah?" Shani asked.

"I wanted to be, but Pega-Soos and I had another job to do that night. Gorgias in his wandering would come upon small villages that would have no defense against him. He would capture anyone he could sell for a slave, and kill the rest. We had to warn the folk, and only Pega-Soos could reach them in time.

"We went from village to village. Pega-Soos swooped low around the houses while I kept shouting that everyone must leave at once and hide in the hills. Sometimes Gorgias was so close behind us that we could hear his men tramping along. Everyone got away in time. Gorgias did not manage to harm a single Jew that night.

"Finally, he gave up and turned back to Emmaus. Of course he hadn't an inkling that Judah had captured it. He finally got the idea when he saw the smoke from Nicanor's burning camp, and Judah's men holding the plain. That's when Gorgias fled, too.

"The enemy had abandoned loads of their weapons. Judah made good use of all those swords and spears and shields, to equip the men who came flocking to join him.

"And, by the way, when the slave-traders ran away they didn't even take their gold and silver. Judah shared it out, especially to the wounded and to widows and orphans."

"Was that when the Maccabees liberated the Temple?" Shani asked.

"No, not yet. The next year, the King's chief minister invaded the land with 60,000 soldiers. By that time, Judah had 10,000. That was when he won his greatest victory of all.

"After that, he was at last able to enter Jerusalem and purify the Temple, and celebrate the first Hanukkah. Do you know what the word *Hanukkah* really means, Shani?"

"Yes, I do. It means *dedication.* Abba explained that to me a long time ago. He wanted me to understand that Hanukkah is about much more than just getting presents."

"Well, now you know what kind of *dedication* it took from the Maccabees and everyone who followed them."

He stroked Pega-Soos, and ruffled his mane.

"We won't forget those days, will we, old friend?"

Pega-Soos tossed his mane and gave a proud neigh.

*Chapter 14*

# The Treasure Hunt

After Elizur and Pega-Soos went on their way, Shani asked, "What are we doing today?"

"Going on a treasure hunt!" the twins exclaimed together.

"Good! Where do we start?"

"At our sukkah," Shamor answered.

Shani expected a grand sukkah, much bigger than the one at home or even at the synagogue, decorated with fresh leaves and fruits and pictures. She could not hide her disappointment when she found it was very small and very old. There were no decorations, and actually it was quite shabby and broken down.

Her friends saw her feelings. "This is no ordinary sukkah, Shani," Zachor explained. "It is one of the first ones built by the Children of Israel who had just escaped from Egypt and were wandering in the wilderness."

When Shani heard that, she looked at it more carefully. An earthenware jug lay in a corner and she thought it too looked very, very old. Shamor brought it to her.

"Find what's inside."

She felt around in the jug and pulled out a rolled-up piece of parchment, with markings in faded ink. They looked like letters, but she could not read a single one of them.

"Is this writing?" she asked.

"It's ancient Hebrew," Shamor said. "So ancient it does not look anything like the letters we read and write today."

I'm sure you two can read it," Shani said. "Please, please tell me what it says."

Zachor took the scroll and tried — not very successfully — to make her voice deep and solemn as she spoke the words.

> *I am Jeremiah son of Hilkiah, a priest of Anathoth. I*
> *foresee that the Temple of Jerusalem will soon be burnt by*
> *Nebuchadnezzar, King of Babylon. Its most precious*
> *Treasure must be saved. I have asked the High Priest to let*
> *me hide it away. I have given it to Elijah the Prophet for*
> *safekeeping. I pray the day will come when it is restored*
> *to the Children of Israel.*

"What is the Treasure? Where is it hidden?"

"The answers are in the hunt," Shamor told her.

"Here is the first clue." Zachor gave her a slip of paper.

### Put together sixty and twenty and twenty.

Of course, sixty and twenty and twenty make one hundred. But one hundred of what? Perhaps the answer was not as easy as it first seemed. Shani had to think hard for a while. Then she remembered something. When her grandfather had first taught her the Hebrew

101

alphabet, he had explained that each letter could be read as either a sound or a number. For example, he had shown her how the second letter, called *"bet,"* could mean either the sound "b" or the number "2." If letters could be numbers, then numbers could be letters.

She began to count off the letters. *"Samekh"* is "sixty" and *"kaf"* is "twenty." In the puzzle, the "twenty" was written twice. She sounded it out — *s-kh-kh*.

She frowned with the effort to make sense of it. Then she had another flash of memory. Her teacher was taking the class through the school sukkah and telling the names of its parts. *"S'khakh"* is the thatch on the partly open roof.

There was a wooden stool in the sukkah. She climbed onto it cautiously, because it looked rather rickety. She could just reach into the thatch, where she found another slip of paper.

### *Go to the tree where Deborah sat when she judged the people.*

She knew the story of Deborah, but could not recall the name of the tree. She had to go back to the palace, where there was a fine library. Once she had a Bible, she soon learned that Deborah sat under a palm tree.

"That's easy to remember when I'm wearing this," she thought, touching King Joseph's gift. "I'd better take a Bible with me. There may be more clues in it." She selected one small enough to carry easily.

This time she took the lead and the twins followed her. Outside in the garden there were small palm trees and medium-sized ones and just one that was very tall and broad. Shani went straight to it, and easily found the next slip of paper in a hollow in the trunk.

*Take one of my branches. Go to the brook.*
*Find there a branch that goes together with my branch.*

How was she ever to work out this one? She had passed a brook several times in the last few days, and she decided to go to it. Perhaps an idea would come to her there. When the girls were seated on the grass beside the brook, Shani stared into the stream and thought and thought. What goes with a palm branch? She saw a picture in her mind of palm branches held upright . . . palm branches waving . . . Abba walking in the Sukkoth procession carrying palm and willow . . .

She jumped up. "A willow! I know willows grow near water. There must be one close by."

She looked upstream and downstream. Sure enough, there was a willow tree, leaning over the brook. The next slip of paper was hanging on the tip of a low branch.

*Find the third that goes with these two.*
*It sounds like one of the names of Queen Esther.*

She could not remember the third branch that Abba carried on Sukkoth, but she was sure it was not called Esther. She took the Bible she had brought from the palace library and turned to the Book of Esther. It was hard to read and understand, but finally she found what she sought. Queen Esther's Hebrew name was Hadassah.

"If it sounds *like* Hadassah, then it isn't exactly the same as Hadassah," she decided. "And it's something with branches."

She wandered among the flowers and shrubs and trees, hoping to recognize the one that she had seen Abba and the other men carry in the proud *lulav*. One shrub had a delicious aroma that drew her to it, almost as though it were calling her. As she bent over to touch the dark leaves and white flowers, the twins came running up to her.

"You've found the *hadas!*" Shamor cried in delight.

"It was only a guess," Shani told them honestly. "I really didn't know. This is called *hadas?*"

"Yes, in Hebrew. In English it's called myrtle."

Tied to a twig of the shrub was another slip of paper.

## *Walk in the direction of the first shake of the lulav. Take as many paces as there are cubits in the length of King Solomon's Temple.*

Shani sighed. "It's so complicated."

She knew, because she always watched eagerly, that the *lulav* was waved first toward the wall where the Ark stood. That meant in the direction of Jerusalem. At home that was eastward, but in Beyond-Sambatyon what was the right direction? She might have to try them all. And how far should she go?

She had to sit down and leaf through her Bible. It was quite a while before she came to King Solomon, and quite a while longer before she found the right figure, but at last she came to it. The length of the Temple was sixty cubits.

She decided not to choose a direction, but just start off the way she happened to be facing. She thought paces should be bigger than mere steps, so she took long strides. At the end of the sixty paces, she was standing right in front of a bush. She quickly found the paper hidden among its leaves.

***Turn in the direction of the journey of the brothers.***
***Count to "qoph."***
***Find the door, and go on to the Treasure.***

What brothers went on a journey? The brothers of Joseph, who went down into Egypt? They traveled southward. She reckoned out that the letter *qoph* equals "one hundred," so she turned to the south and counted one hundred paces.

She was so intent on looking down at the ground and measuring her way, that she did not notice Shamor and Zachor slip ahead of her. Only when she finished the steps and looked up did she see them waiting for her. They were standing close together, but when she reached them they moved apart.

Behind them was a slope of earth covered with a tangle of thick vines. Shani stepped up to it, pulled aside the vines. They had completely hidden a narrow opening cut into the soil of the hill-side.

Shamor and Zachor each gave her a hug and a kiss. They were so excited that they kept interrupting one another.

"You've shown how bright you are . . . "

"How much you have learned . . ."

"You don't give up . . ."

"Now you'll have your reward . . ."

"You'll never forget it . . ."

"Have I solved all the clues?" Shani asked.

"Yes, you have."

"Did you two make them all up by yourselves?"

"Machshavah helped."

"Now we can go on to the Treasure," the twins gestured together toward the opening.

"Where does it go? Is it another tunnel?" Shani tried not to sound reluctant.

"No. There are chambers built into the hill."

They went single file through the opening, into a narrow passage that had walls lined with rough-hewn stone. It was short, but it turned and twisted at sharp angles. Then they came out into a chamber with the same kind of walls. Shamor took an oil lamp from a stand near the threshold and lit it. It gave just enough light to guide them across the earthen floor to the far wall, where there was another narrow opening.

"The next chamber is guarded by the Wolf of Benjamin," Zachor said. "Do not fear him."

They went through the opening and along another short twisted passage into the second chamber. A huge wolf crouched across the threshold. He bristled his thick gray fur and growled from deep within his broad chest. The twins spoke quietly to him, and he padded aside to let them pass.

Shani tried not to tremble as she entered the chamber, with Shamor ahead of her and Zachor behind her. They crossed the room to the far wall, where there was still another narrow opening.

"The next chamber is guarded by the Lion of Judah," Shamor said. "Do not fear him."

They went through the opening and along another short twisted passage into the third chamber. A huge lion crouched across the threshold. He tossed his heavy tawny mane and gave a roar that echoed from the stone walls. The twins spoke quietly to him, and he padded aside to let them pass.

Shani felt a little more confident now, and again walked forward between her friends. They crossed the room to the far wall, where there was still another narrow opening.

"The last chamber is guarded by seraphim with flaming swords," Zachor said. "Do not fear them."

They went through the opening and along another short twisted passage into the last chamber. On either side of the threshold there was a seraph. Each was very tall, and each had six large wings. They gleamed and sparked with a fiery glow, and held aloft swords with blades that blazed like flames. Even though she had been warned, Shani gasped and jumped back. Then she took a deep breath and held it as the girls passed one by one between the seraphim.

The walls of this chamber were made of sapphire and amethyst, that seemed to have lights deep within them. The floor was marble. At the far of the chamber, there was a deep niche cut into the wall, shielded with a grill of fine gold mesh.

Shani felt a thrill she could not describe even before she looked into the niche. When she did look, she was too stunned to speak. Resting in the niche were two Tablets cut from stone, inscribed with words she could not read. She knew without asking that this was more of the most ancient Hebrew writing. She knew without asking what words these were.

When she found her voice, she whispered. "The Treasure. The Treasure from the Temple."

"Yes," Shamor and Zachor spoke together, also in awed whispers. They went on, taking turns.

"The greatest of all Treasures."

"The Tablets of the Covenant."

"The Tablets that Moses brought down from Mount Sinai."

Pieces of broken stone were scattered in the niche. Zachor noticed Shani looking at them and said, "Those are the first Tablets, that Moses smashed in his rage when the people danced around the golden calf."

Shani felt that she could never gaze long enough. When the twins told her it was time to go, she could scarcely force herself to turn away, and she kept looking back again and again. She felt both happy and sad as they made their way out, past the seraphim, the lion and the wolf. She was happy that she had seen the Treasure, and sad that she would never see it again. She was happy that it still existed, and sad that it was kept hidden away here in the secret chamber.

"Will it ever be given back to us?" she wondered.

❧ ❧ ❧

Queen Shabbat listened with grave attention when her daughters told her the tale of the day's adventures. They told her how Shani had worked out each clue, no matter how puzzling it was. They told her how she had braved the wolf and the lion and the fiery seraphim to reach her goal.

When they had done, the Queen smiled and looked toward Prince Lecha-Dodi, who had also been listening. He smiled, too, and they nodded to one another.

When Shani saw this, she felt she had passed a test.

Chapter 15

# Af-Bri

The next morning, Queen Shabbat took Shani alone to her private parlor.

"I think you can guess what I have to tell you."

"Is it time to go to Af-Bri?"

"Yes, my dear. It is time."

"How can I find him?"

"On the highest peak of the highest mountain in Beyond-Sambatyon. There is only one road up that mountain, and it is a very hard one. Shamor and Zachor will show you were it starts. Then you must go on alone. They cannot go with you."

Shani was disappointed to hear that, but she put on a brave face and said, "I'll go. Elijah told me to."

"You have the mirror I gave you. If you are frightened or weary or down at heart, look into it. You will find your courage in it. You may borrow this cloak, you will need it along the way."

The garment was made of coarse wool, very worn and shabby. It was out of place among the fine things in the palace, but somehow it seemed familiar to her.

"I'll never let go of them. I promise."

"Do you always keep your promises, Shani?"

The question made her uneasy. She knew she had to tell the truth to the Queen.

"I always mean to."

Queen Shabbat gazed at her steadily and said nothing. Shani went on, "Once, lately, I forgot to."

"Would you like to tell me about it?"

"It was last term in school. There was a new girl in the class. Her name is Bernice. In an arithmetic test, I saw that she was looking at my answers and copying them."

She paused. The Queen still did not speak, so she went on.

"Afterwards, during recess, Bernice said that if I promised never to tell anyone what she did, she would promise never, ever to cheat again. I said that was all right."

"Did you keep your promise?"

"I really did mean to," Shani said unhappily. "But one day in the playground we argued about the rules of a game. I got mad at her, and in front of all the other girls I said how I knew she cheated. She ran away crying. She never spoke to me again."

Shani was crying herself now. The Queen drew her close and wiped away the tears.

"When you get home, you are going to tell Bernice how sorry you are, aren't you?"

Shani nodded. "I promise."

"That promise I am sure you will keep."

Shani nodded again. She could not imagine breaking her word to Queen Shabbat.

The Queen took Shani as far as the gates of the palace, where Shamor and Zachor were waiting.

**ea ea ea**

It was a long walk to the lowest slope of Af-Bri's mountain, but Shani was too excited to get tired.

"This is as far as we can go with you," Zachor told her.

"We'll be waiting for you when you come back," Shamor assured her.

She took the lunch basket they had brought for her, and with a quick farewell to the twins, she started on her way alone.

At first the climb was pleasant. The path was wide and inclined gently upward. On either side the grass was thick, and leafy trees gave shade from the sun. Many kinds of birds perched on the branches, and some took to the air to flutter along with her, singing merry songs.

As she went higher, the path grew narrower and steeper. The grass was sparse, and then gone altogether. The trees were fewer and smaller. By and by, they too were gone. On either side of her was hard brown earth with scattered bare rocks. There were no more birds to cheer her with their melody.

The sky turned from blue to gray, and dark clouds hid the sun. The air turned chilly. Winds whipped at her. She unfolded the cloak and wrapped it around her. It covered her completely and kept her comfortably warm.

As she went ever higher, the path became ever steeper. Soon it was not a path at all, but only a crooked lane twisting between boulders bigger than she was. Once she stumbled over a stone and fell, but was not hurt. A little way farther on, the boulders closed in front of her. There was no way to pass between them.

"Will I have to go back? Will I have to say I couldn't do it?"

She sat and thought. She took the mirror from her pocket, looked into it and at first she saw only her own face. The longer she looked, the more faces she saw — Queen Shabbat — the twins — Ima and Abba, with the loving looks she saw when they kissed her goodnight — Dani crying fretfully — Cousin Adam sneering, as though to say, "I knew you couldn't do it."

She put the mirror away and started up the path again. Soon she discovered a way between the boulders that she had not before noticed. She followed it until her path was crossed by a stream gushing down a gully. Though there were scarcely any trees on this part of the mountain, one stood leaning over the stream, gnarled and twisted and without leaves. The stretch of water was not wide and did not appear to be deep. Shani was sure she could wade through it.

When she was halfway across to the other side, a rush of water hit her and knocked her over into the foam. She screamed and thrashed, trying to keep herself from being swept away. Then she felt something solid in her grasp. It was a thick, rope-like root of the tree, thrusting over the edge of the gully. Clinging tightly to it, Shani pulled herself back to the stony ground she had just left.

She sat there clutching the trunk of the tree and — since there was nobody to see or hear her — she sobbed until the fright began to fade. Then she took off the wet cloak and found that it had protected her so well that her clothes were not even damp. Most important, the mirror was safe in her pocket.

Shani looked into the mirror again. She saw her house, with the parched ground around it, and then the rest of the neighborhood, with dusty earth and wilted stalks where usually there were beds of blooming flowers. It reminded her how important it was to reach Af-Bri.

"I can't give up. I won't give up."

While she looked into the mirror the scene changed. It still showed the stream, but not at the spot where she was sitting. The bare tree and her own figure were not in the center but in a far corner. In the center was a row of round flat stones running from one side of the stream to the other. She jumped up and walked along the bank until she came to the stones she had seen in the mirror. Very carefully, she stepped from one to another until she was across without having to go into the water at all.

Her spirits rose and she went on. It had gotten much colder, but she was cozy within the folds of the cloak that was already dry. Yet the way was very hard, and she was very tired.

"I'll sit down and rest a minute," she decided.

While she was looking for a good place to sit, it began to snow. At first, large flakes floated down softly, then heavier and heavier, blown in swirls by a howling wind. It was a real blizzard, and she could not see through it. She did not dare take out the mirror, lest it be snatched from her in the blast.

She trudged on, the snow piling up around her, until she came to a low, broad rock. Behind it was a crag and above it an overhanging ledge that formed a nook sheltered from the storm. Thankfully, Shani crawled into the nook and huddled as far back as she could get. She shook the snow from the cloak and closed it snugly around her. It seemed safe enough here to take the mirror from her pocket for another look.

At first she saw the same sight that was all around her. Little by little, it changed. The dismal dark gray sky turned a clear light blue.

The lowering black clouds turned to delicate white puffs. The grim rock cliffs blossomed with green vines and flowers of many hues.

"This must be dreamland," she thought as she drifted toward sleep. The lovely picture in the mirror merged into her dream until she could not tell them apart.

When Shani awoke the blizzard was over. The sky was bright, and the sun was melting what was left of the snow. This was a good time and place to eat her lunch. Feeling rested and cheerful after her nap and her meal, she left the nook and took up her route. As the mountain rose, it became narrower and narrower, as though it were coming to a peak.

"It can't be much farther," she told herself. "Soon I'll find Af-Bri."

At that moment there came a roaring noise. Chunks of rock were rolling and pounding down the mountainside straight toward her. She skipped aside as they hurtled past. Some bounced off the hard ground. A few even shot up and hit her, but as soon as they touched the cloak they fell away and did her no harm. She was sure by now that it was no ordinary garment that Queen Shabbat had loaned to her.

"This time it really can't be much farther."

This time she was right. She had come to the top of the mountain and onto a circle of almost level ground. There was a rim of low hills all around it, and above each hill was a ball of cloud. Streams of rain from the clouds ran down the hillsides like waterfalls.

Standing before the highest hill was someone so tall that she had to strain to look all the way up to him. Wild locks of hair blew around his head, and rivulets of water dripped down his long beard. He held a streak of forked lightning and waved it like a baton as he chanted in a booming bass voice.

115

*Rains go flow,*
*Winds go blow,*
*Toss and tumble!*

*Lightning flash,*
*Thunder crash,*
*Roar and rumble!*

As Shani watched from the edge of the circle, he pointed to the east and a cluster of sodden clouds scuttled off. He gestured to the south and a gust of wind shot off. Although she felt uncertain and even nervous, she could not help thinking of a policeman directing traffic and had to hold back a giggle.

Before she approached him she took a look into the mirror, but it showed only her own face.

"That means I'm on my own."

She smoothed her tousled hair, straightened the folds of the cloak and stepped forward.

"Excuse me, please. Are you His Highness Af-Bri?"

She had decided this would be a suitable form of address for the Prince of the Rains and Winds, and surely this giant personage was high enough.

He scarcely glanced at her as he went on with his conducting, but he did speak.

"You are a very stubborn child. I expected you would give up and go back. Why do you come to disturb me at my work?"

"Please don't be angry. Elijah the Prophet sent me."

At that he turned to her, and looked less severe.

"And Queen Shabbat told me where to find you."

"If that's so, I suppose I can spare you a minute or two. What do you want?"

"Rain. Where I come from, it hasn't rained for months and months. Everything is all dried up. Even the rivers. Nothing grows, and the farmers lost their crops. The reservoirs are almost empty. Soon there won't even be water to drink. Please, Prince Af-Bri, help us. Elijah said you can."

Af-Bri stared hard at her. "Keep quiet and let me think about it."

He went back to directing the rain clouds and the winds for so long that Shani began to wonder if he had forgotten her. She was afraid that if she spoke up he would be annoyed, so she waited quietly. Finally he turned back to her.

"Go home and tell this to your people there. Tell them I promise to send rain their way, but only if they remember all their own promises and keep them. Especially the ones they forgot. If they keep their promises, I will keep mine."

Shani drew a deep breath of relief.

"Thank you very much, Prince Af-Bri."

She looked up at him, towering above her. With a wave of his lightning baton he stirred up a gale wind and sent it flying. He twirled the baton and there was a growl of thunder. He pointed to a clump of dark cloud and it split into four parts that scudded away to carry their load of rain in each direction.

"Well, what are you waiting for, child? Can't you see I have my work to do? And you have yours."

"Yes, Prince Af-Bri. I know what to do. Goodbye."

The way back down was much easier than the tough climb up to the peak. Shani was so light of heart now that she skipped and danced as she went. By the time she reached the bottom it was almost evening. Shamor and Zachor, who had stayed awaiting her all this time, were overjoyed that she had fulfilled her mission and come safely back.

Before it was dark, the three girls were home in the palace. Queen Shabbat herself stood at the bronze gates to welcome them.

"I'm very proud of you, Shani," she said, embracing her. "You've been as brave and steadfast as I believed you would be."

"I couldn't have been without the mirror," Shani said earnestly. "And this cloak. I think it must be something special, because nothing could harm me while I wore it."

"It is indeed special. This is the famous mantle of Elijah. He left it here so you could use it."

At that, Shani stroked the worn wool before she gave it back to Queen Shabbat. She also gave a yawn she could not hide.

"I see that now you need a good supper and a good night's sleep. You have certainly earned them."

## Chapter 16

## Farewell to Beyond-Sambatyon

The next morning, Shani dressed in the same clothes that she had worn on her journey to Beyond-Sambatyon. She also wore the chain with the palm-tree pendant that was the gift of King Joseph. In a basket with a lid she packed the mirror, the doll with the ruby eyes and the golden apple. There was quite a bit of space left in the basket, but she had nothing else to put in it. She had just finished when Shamor and Zachor came in.

"I'll miss you both so much," she said, the tears beginning to come. "Won't we ever be together again?"

"Whenever Shabbat candles are lit, we will be together."

"That will be always," Shani said with certainty.

"All Jews used to rejoice in Shabbat," Zachor said sadly. "Now, many of them don't even remember it or care about it."

"We try to bring it to every home," Shamor said, just as sadly. "More and more, we are shut out."

"I'll never shut you out."

At that the twins smiled. They had been holding something behind them, that they brought out and held forth.

"We made this for you ourselves."

It was a challah cover of the purest white linen, exquisitely embroidered in silken threads of many colors. In the center, the word *SHABBAT* was skillfully stitched.

"How gorgeous. Did you really make it yourselves?"

"When you're a grown-up lady and have it in your own home, it will remind you of us."

"But won't we ever meet for real? To talk, and play and have adventures together?"

"Who knows? You've found out that remarkable things can happen in Beyond-Sambatyon."

Shani decided to ask the twins a question that had been on her mind since she first met them.

"How old are you really? You don't seem any older than I am, but you know so much."

They looked thoughtful and serious when they gave their answer. Zachor spoke first.

"I know it is hard to believe, but we came into being on the seventh day after Creation. As long as Jews continue to Observe and Remember Shabbat, we will be eternally young."

"If ever the Jews forget, and discard Shabbat," Shamor said, "then we will wither and crumble away."

"Now, if you're ready, come along. Our Mother is waiting for you."

Shani took a last look around the room where she had come to feel so much at home. "Goodbye," she whispered to it before she left.

Queen Shabbat was in her reception room, and so were some of Shani's new friends.

Prince Lecha-Dodi came up to her, holding a pair of very handsomely wrought candlesticks. "Please take these as a gift for your Ima, who has always received us so graciously."

He wrapped them in a suede cloth and put them into her basket, as Shani shyly stammered her thanks.

Next, His Excellency Havdalah came forth and presented a carved case holding a *havdalah* set with candlestick and spice box. "Please take this as a gift for your Abba, who has always given his family the gift of Shabbat."

Before Shani had finished thanking him, he stepped back and Prince Kiddush took his place. His gift was a kiddush cup engraved with the words of the blessing for wine. "This is for your brother Dani. Take care of it for him, and give it to him when he is grown up."

He had barely put it into the basket when Madam Cholent waddled up. She held out a stiff parchment envelope sealed with a blob of wax. "I never gave this to anyone until now. It's the full recipe for my original and only true cholent. Follow it exactly and don't change a pinch of anything."

"I will," Shani promised. "I mean, I won't. I mean, I'll do exactly what it says."

"You may give it to your own daughters one day, but nobody else. You're a nice child. I wish you good appetite."

Next came Machshavah and Ma'aseh, together holding a scrapbook.

Ma'aseh told her, "Machshavah put together pictures and maps of Beyond-Sambatyon, and essays about it."

Machshavah told her, "Ma'aseh mounted everything and bound it in this cover with a cord and tassel."

Shani took the scrapbook. "I'm glad you both did it. It's a perfect souvenir of my visit."

Last of all, Queen Shabbat rose from her chair and Shani approached her. Her gift was a challah plate of porcelain so fine that the light shone through it. The blessing for bread was painted in delicate letters around the rim.

"Something to go under the cover my children made for you," she said, with a twinkle of merriment in her smile.

Shani was afraid to touch anything so fragile, until the Queen assured her, "We know how to make porcelain that does not break. It is very hard to make, so we use it only for very special things. This plate can be an heirloom from generation to generation. Only if it is no longer used as it was meant to be, then it will crack and crumble."

Shani could hardly think of anything to say, as the Queen wrapped the plate in a silk bag. It just fit into the basket, that was almost entirely filled.

"I will take you home myself," the Queen told her. "We must leave now."

Shani turned to her friends. "Thank you all for such a wonderful visit. I'll never forget a minute of it. I'll miss you all dreadfully."

Shamor and Zachor quickly kissed her once more and Madam Cholent gave her a massive hug. She wiped away some tears, waved and hurried after Queen Shabbat.

🐚 🐚 🐚

Pega-Soos was waiting for them on the broad lawn behind the palace. This time he was hitched not to the small ancient chariot in which Elizur sometimes rode, but to a large white one with two pairs of broad wings and cushioned seats under a canopy.

Shani stroked him and whispered, "I'm sure you could talk if you wanted to, but you don't need to, do you?" He whinnied and bobbed his head slightly. She thought he gave her a look both wise and amused.

Elizur was standing next to the chariot, to help them up. The Queen stepped in first and as Shani was about to follow, he casually held out something wrapped in a piece of coarse cloth.

"I thought maybe you'd like to have this. It's just a plain old clay oil lamp. We had it in our house in Zarephath when Elijah first came to us there. I guess that makes it a sort of a memento. If any time you don't have electricity, this will still work and give you light."

"Thank you so much, Elizur. I've always wanted to have something from those ancient days. This is the best of all." She tucked it into the last space left in the basket. Then he gave her a boost up to her seat, and jogged off across the lawn.

Pega-Soos was just starting off at an easy trot when they heard a loud bray not far off. At a word from the Queen, Pega-Soos halted and they watched the arrival of a quite remarkable little band.

Balaam's she-ass was clopping along at a surprisingly fast pace, braying as she went as though to let Shani know that she was coming. Noah was sitting astride her back, with Chad Gadya curled up in front of him. The raven and the dove fluttered just above them. Alongside the she-ass, the two apes from Ophir were leaping and bounding, turning somersaults and cartwheels.

"Ahoy, there!" Noah shouted. "Weren't you going to wait for us to see you off?"

"We didn't know you were coming," Shani said. "But I'm so glad you did. All of you!"

"I heard that you were going home today," the raven said. "I flew right to the Captain to report to him."

"You only heard about it," the dove said. "I actually saw Her Majesty leave the palace with Shani, and told you all to hurry."

The she-ass snapped at them, "Stop bickering and say something nice for a change."

The two birds for a moment seemed stunned at this command.

Then the raven said, "I like having Shani here."

The dove said, "Me, too. I wish she would stay longer."

The raven said, "I wish she would stay forever."

The dove said, "Me, too."

They stared at each other in amazement. They could not disagree!

Noah now opened a sack and brought forth his *kinor*.

"We will perform a serenade just for you," he told Shani.

He strummed his instrument, and they all began to sing. Noah was off-key. The she-ass produced a rough sound and Chad Gadya a squeaky one. The apes came in with deep basso tones, and continued their acrobatics even as they sang. The raven and the dove cawed and cooed the words, and accompanied their renditions with decorative swoops and loops in the air. No one in this chorus was quite in time with any of the others.

> *Oh, our Shani dear,*
> *We're sad to hear*
> *That this is the day*
> *When you go your way.*

*We loved to meet you,*
*We loved to greet you,*
*We feel it grievous*
*That you should leave us.*

*So we come to croon*
*This beautiful tune,*
*As our way to tell*
*You our fond farewell.*

*But only for now,*
*'Cause sometime, somehow,*
*We'll see you once more*
*On Sambatyon's shore.*

They did not all finish together, but at the end they all gave a deep sigh together and as a final flourish the apes did a couple of spectacular backflips. Shani jumped down from the chariot and ran to them. She gave each a hug, except the birds whom she petted lest a hug crush them.

"Don't forget us," Chad Gadya pleaded.

"As if I ever could!"

She turned back toward the carriage, wiping away tears of sorrow and laughter. Once more she took her seat beside the Queen, and Pega-Soos drew the chariot into the air. In moments they were above the River PaGaHaP, still flying low enough for Shani to see a familiar pair of creatures in midstream. Baby Leviathan was swimming along with the current with Behemoth sitting on his back, working hard to keep his balance.

As the chariot passed by, Baby wagged his gleaming tail vigorously and called "Hello, Shani! We're finally on our way to that island. Where are you going?"

"I'm going home," she called back.

"If you ever take a sea voyage, look around for me. Goodbye, Shani!"

Behemoth bellowed, "Good luck to you, little one."

Shani was surprised at hearing anything friendly from him. She answered warmly, "Thank you, Behemoth."

Pega-Soos now rose higher, and was soon skimming above the great cliff and the waterfall. On the other side of the cliff were Asher and Gad and Dan, mounted on their horses, as though they had been expecting her. The chariot was now too far from the ground for Shani to hear their voices, but she could see them wave and leaned over the side to wave back.

When they were up among the clouds the air turned chilly and Queen Shabbat wrapped a fold of her own cloak around Shani. A sharp wind blew so strongly that the chariot rocked. Pega-Soos had to struggle harder and harder to keep them steady and on course, as they were tossed up and down.

Black clouds blew in on the gale and closed around them. Jagged streaks of lightning flashed in a chain one after another, followed by rolling claps of thunder. Icy sleet fell all around them, but never quite touched them.

Shani told herself that in the company of Queen Shabbat she must be safe. She huddled close to her, and looked up to her for reassurance. The Queen smiled at her calmly.

"There's nothing to fear. I told you once that Af-Bri is an odd creature. This is his way of letting you know that he is keeping you in mind. I imagine that it's his notion of humor. It will be over very soon."

In a few minutes, the storm was indeed over and the sky was again clear. Shani looked down and discovered that while they had been wrapped in dark clouds they had flown over the River Sambatyon and the Land of Beyond-Sambatyon was now far behind her.

First she felt sorry that she was gone from that wonderful place and the friends she had made there. Then, her feelings changed quickly to eagerness to be home. She felt that she could scarcely bear to be separated from Ima and Abba and Dani any longer. Warm and cozy, lulled by the gentle sway of the flying chariot, she drifted into daydreams about her memories and her hopes.

She was jolted back to reality by the light bump of landing. Queen Shabbat kissed her and set her down near the very spot where she had waited for Duchipat. Then Pega-Soos flew so swiftly and so high that anyone else who saw the chariot in the sky would have mistaken it for a cloud.

She looked around. Home was as it had always been, but after her adventures it seemed almost strange. It was still very hot. A blazing orange sun was near to setting. Everything seemed even more dry and withered and cracked than before.

Then she heard her own name cried aloud. She looked toward the house and saw Ima and Abba running toward her as fast as they could, waving and calling as they ran.

*Chapter 17*

# Home Again

S he was grasped and hugged tightly and kissed again and again by both of them at once.

"Shani, Shani, my darling girl," Ima said over and over, crying as she said it.

"Where have you been?" Abba shouted at her as though he were very angry, but he was crying too. "Where did you go? Where have you been? How could you do this to us?"

"I've been in the Land of Beyond-Sambatyon," she said, wondering why they were so upset. "I told you I was going there. You said I could go, I remember for sure."

"But that was just a game you were playing," Ima exclaimed, still hugging her.

"You went off early this morning and stayed away the whole day," Abba said. "We've been searching everywhere, and asking everyone who might have seen you."

"It wasn't this morning..." she broke off in confusion. Was it possible that a whole week had passed in Beyond-Sambatyon while it was still the same day at home? "But why did you worry? I told you that Elijah the Prophet would look after me. So did Queen Shabbat, and my friends . . ."

"Stop that fooling," Abba said sternly. "You must tell us where you went when you ran away."

"I didn't . . . I told you . . ." She did not know how to make them believe. Then she noticed the basket that Queen Shabbat had set down beside her.

"All these things are from Beyond-Sambatyon. Just look."

"Later," Abba said. "Come into the house."

"I'm coming," she said meekly. But she was laughing to herself at the surprises she had for them.

৵ ৵ ৵

When she began to tell them about Queen Shabbat, Shamor and Zachor and all the others, they listened in bewilderment.

Finally, Abba said, "First we will get ready for Shabbat dinner, and give thanks that you are safe home with us. Then you'll tell us the truth."

As they sang *Shalom Aleichem,* Shani gazed at the flickering flames of the candles. For a moment it seemed to her that the little wisps hovering over them were not smoke but angelic forms. When they came to *Tzetchem LeShalom* she blinked, and when she looked again they were gone.

৵ ৵ ৵

At breakfast the next morning Shani sat beside Dani's highchair and told him about Baby Leviathan. Perhaps he understood, because he chuckled.

Ima and Abba were studying the gifts in the basket, exclaiming at their beauty but very puzzled by them.

"Where did you get these things?" Abba demanded.

"I told you, Abba. The plate is a present from Queen Shabbat, and the candlesticks from Prince Lecha-Dodi, and . . ."

"That's make-believe," he interrupted. "Where have you really been and where did you really get them?"

"It's all true, I promise!" She was close to tears because she could not make them understand.

Ima spoke softly to Abba. "Let it be now, dear. We have to leave for the synagogue."

"I must tell everybody there the message from Af-Bri," Shani told them, feeling awkward about it.

Ima started to say, "Don't act silly . . ." Then she hesitated, "Everyone was so worried about you."

🐦 🐦 🐦

The people in the congregation seemed even more depressed than before. They were relieved to know that Shani had come home, but otherwise they were weary and listless. Only when they prayed for rain did they raise their voices.

Shani looked about for Miriam, but she was not there. That was disappointing. Miriam surely would believe every word of her story, even if nobody else did. She saw Bernice at the other side of the room.

The first person to come up to them was Mrs. Jacobs.

"You naughty girl," she scolded. "To run away and drive your poor parents frantic."

Ima broke in. "All's well that ends well, Mrs. Jacobs. Let's not talk about it anymore, please."

Others had gathered around, curious and asking questions. Now was the time to give them Af-Bri's message, but how could she speak out to all these grown-ups? She felt so shy and unsure of herself, she could not do it. Then she remembered what to do. She took a quick glance into Queen Shabbat's mirror and saw her own figure trudging up the stony mountain.

"If I could do that, I can do this," she told herself. Then, still shyly, she said, "Please, everybody! There is something important that I have to tell you!"

The men and women and children, who had not been talking much, turned to look at her. Even the rabbi and the hazzan paid attention.

"I have been to the Land of Beyond-Sambatyon," she began. "Elijah the Prophet told me how to get there, to find out why it hasn't rained for so long."

Some laughed, some just turned away. Shani knew they thought she was telling a story. If Shamor and Zachor were with her she would not be afraid to go on, so she pretended they were and went on.

"Do you remember Af-Bri? His name is in the service for Shemini Atzeret." She looked to the rabbi to confirm this.

"That's right," he said. "There is a passage that says Af-Bri is the Prince of Rain. And there is a plea that rain will not be held back because promises have been forgotten."

Shani felt encouraged by that, and went on. "Af-Bri takes promises very seriously. I know, because I found him on a mountaintop in Beyond-Sambatyon and talked to him. He says he will send us rain if we keep all our promises."

There were some murmurs and whisperings, but nobody gave an answer. Shani looked straight at Bernice and said, "I know it's a very bad thing to break a promise. It hurts other people and makes all kinds of trouble. I did it to somebody, and I'm terribly sorry. I wish that person would forgive me."

Bernice broke into a big smile. She stood up before she spoke, as though she were in a schoolroom. "I promised my Mother not to eat so much chocolate, but I buy it with money from my allowance and hide it and eat it in secret. That's being sneaky. If that makes Af-Bri angry, I won't do it anymore."

Miss Levi, the teacher of their class, looked from one to another of her pupils.

"I must say that I'm learning something from my students. Twice I promised my class to work out new and more interesting lessons. But I never got around to it. When school opens in the fall there'll be a lot of changes made. This time I mean it."

The murmurs were louder now, all of them approving — especially from the children.

A portly gentleman stepped forward. He was the town's Commissioner of Public Works.

"I wish to tell about something that disturbs me deeply. There had been complaints about a hole in a sidewalk. I kept promising to inspect it and have it fixed. But I kept putting it off, because I was very busy and had a lot of work to finish before I went away on vacation. Because I neglected my duty, an elderly lady fell there and was hurt so badly that she had to be taken to the hospital. She is recovering now, thank heaven, but it's my fault that she suffered injury and pain and fright."

To Shani's surprise, her own father spoke up next.

"I know about that accident. It took too long for an ambulance to come for her, because there are never enough drivers for emergencies. A friend of mine who belongs to the Volunteer Ambulance

Corps keeps asking me to join, and I keep promising that I will when I have time. But I never find the time. I'll sign up tomorrow."

Mr. and Mrs. Roth, who were quite rich, were been sitting side by side. Now they glanced at one another, Mr. Roth nodded, and Mrs. Roth started to speak.

"Last year when we were in Israel, we went to what they call a development town. There are many new immigrants there, and many of them are poor. They have hard lives. We promised to build a community center for the town, with an auditorium, and a library, and a swimming pool. We even spoke to an architect about designing it." She hesitated and stopped.

"Go on," Mrs. Jacobs ordered. "Is it finished? Why didn't we hear about it?"

"When we got home, we decided that Morty needs a place to relax from business," Mrs. Roth explained. "So we bought a boat. One big enough to take our friends cruising."

"I couldn't afford that and the community center both," Mr. Roth said. He sounded embarrassed. Then his expression changed.

"So we're going to sell the boat. Then we're going to build the community center."

Now the rabbi spoke. "I think the point has been well made by now. We have to thank Shani for waking us up to take a look at ourselves. Let's go home with a lot to think about. We will talk about it again later on."

"I have something to say," Mrs. Jacobs announced.

Some members sighed, and a few groaned.

"I make it a rule for myself to help people all I can. When I see them making mistakes, I tell them so, and how to correct them. It's my duty, for their own good. But I'm beginning to think they don't always understand my kind intentions. I promise that I'll try to be more tactful. I can't promise that I always will be, I only promise to try."

At that, everyone applauded. For the first time ever, they saw Mrs. Jacobs blush.

&#8483; &#8483; &#8483;

As they were walking home, Abba said, "I still don't know what you've been up to Shani, but you were a heroine this morning. I believe we'll all be the better for it. Ima and I are very proud of our little Woman of Valor."

"Thank you, Abba," she said happily. She wanted to tell them again how it had all come about, but not yet. One day, perhaps, they would understand.

Ima said, "I have a promise to keep, too, sweetheart. Often I've meant to spend more time with you, and always put it off because there was so much else to do. From now on, we'll have our special times alone together. On Monday we'll go downtown, just you and me, and have lunch out and shop for your new school clothes."

"And here's a promise from me," Shani said. "Next Shabbat, I'll make an extra special cholent, all by myself. You're not to help or even watch. It will be different from anything you ever tasted."

*Chapter 18*

# Another Visit from Elijah

It was Monday night. Shani was snuggled in her bed, with the doll with the ruby eyes beside her. Through the open windows came only heat and no fresh air or breeze.

She was thinking about the day with Ima. For the first time, they had chosen her new things together. They had lunch in a ladies' tearoom with flowers on the table.

Even in that room cooled by air-conditioning, the flowers seemed wilted and drooping. Would it ever rain, and the heat break?

She fell asleep. Then, somehow, she felt that somebody was in the room with her. She awoke and sat up to find Elijah standing near by. He was grave, as usual, but at the same time he was smiling at her. He seemed pleased.

"You have done very well, Shani. Nothing frightened you off from fulfilling your mission. You were brave to go all the way to Beyond-Sambatyon. You were braver still to find your way to Af-Bri.

You were bravest of all to face those people at your synagogue and get them to listen to you."

"Oh, Elijah, please tell me. Will it do any good? Nothing has happened."

"A lot has happened. Your father has already started to work with the Volunteer Ambulance Corps. Miss Levi is busy with new lessons for her class. Mr. and Mrs. Roth have telephoned an architect in Israel to start the plans for the community center."

Shani thought there was a twinkle under his serious look when he added, "For two days, Mrs. Jacobs hasn't scolded her son. I think Af-Bri will be satisfied. Go back to sleep, my friend Shani, and have sweet dreams."

He was beginning to fade away, and she did not want him to leave her. She tried to think of something to say to keep him there longer, but she was slipping into slumber . . .

She was out in the field behind the house, the place where Duchipat had carried her off and Queen Shabbat had brought her home again. It was no longer bare and parched. There were soft green grass and blossoms of many colors. Fresh water was rising in a sparkling stream, and birds darted about singing mightily. She was playing there, and Shamor and Zachor were playing with her.

She was startled awake by a tremendous crash of noise. For a moment she was confused, before she realized that it was a great clap of thunder and its rolling echo. Heavy rain was dashing in through the open windows. Before she could get up to shut them, Abba came in, flipped on a light switch, and hurried to close the windows and draw the curtains.

Outside in the hallway, Ima was carrying and soothing Dani, who was howling his distress at the terrible racket.

"You're not scared, are you, dear?" Abba asked anxiously. "It's only a rainstorm. Just what we've been praying for."

"Of course I'm not scared Abba. I'm happy as can be."

She imagined Af-Bri on the mountaintop, sending the rainstorm on its way, and laughed at the picture in her mind.

Abba tucked a cover around her and kissed her. Like Elijah, he said, "Go back to sleep, and have sweet dreams."

He went to the door, and looked back as he switched off the light. The doll's ruby eyes glinted in the darkness.

"I wonder," he murmured to himself. "I wonder . . ."

## THE END